Helen M. Winslow

Salome Shepard, Reformer.

Helen M. Winslow

Salome Shepard, Reformer.

ISBN/EAN: 9783337295134

Printed in Europe, USA, Canada, Australia, Japan

Cover: Foto ©Andreas Hilbeck / pixelio.de

More available books at **www.hansebooks.com**

SALOME SHEPARD, REFORMER.

BY

HELEN M. WINSLOW.

BOSTON, MASS.:

Arena Publishing Company,

COPLEY SQUARE,

1893.

ARENA PRESS.

"Pardon, gentles all,

The flat, unraised spirit that hath dared

On this unworthy scaffold to bring forth

So great an object."

Shakespeare.

SALOME SHEPARD, REFORMER.

Salome Shepard gazed wonderingly at the crowd of people in the street, as she guided her pony-phaeton through the factory precincts.

" What can be the matter with these people ? " she thought. " I'm sure they ought to have gone to their work before this."

It was a wet October day. The narrow street was slippery with the muddy water that oozed along to the gutters. The factory boarding-houses loomed up on either side, dingy and desolate. Even the mills looked larger and coarser, in the gloomy air of the morning.

1

As she drove by them, the fair owner listened
in vain for the rumble of machinery. Inside,
the great, well-lighted rooms looked dreary
and barn-like in the gray mist that struggled
through the windows.

One hour before, the machinery, shrieking
and groaning, had voiced the protest of the
" hands " against their fancied and their real
wrongs. One hour before, every employe had
been in his or her place. But the gloom of the
atmosphere could not obscure the suppressed
excitement of the morning. Shortsighted and
blind to their best interest, they might have
been ; but there was not a man among them
who did not feel a tremendous underlying
principle at stake.

And so, at precisely ten o'clock, the machinery
had suddenly and mysteriously stopped, and
every man, woman and child, without a word,
had left the mills.

All this had happened while Salome Shepard
was calling on an elderly friend of her mother's
at the other end of the town. It had been a
delightfully cosy morning in spite of the rain ;
and, after a gossipy fashion, they had passed
it in discussing, as women will, the newest

pattern of crochet, the last society-novel, the coming concerts in town.

Salome's mood was the comfortable one conduced by such soothing intellectual food, as she set forth on her homeward drive. The rain had ceased, and only along the river did the mists hover, suggesting to her idle fancy the thick smoke which hangs over a smouldering fire.

But the fire which had been creeping under the life of the Shawsheen Mills had but just burst into flames, which mounted higher and higher as the day wore on.

All through the factory precincts the unwonted excitement was manifest. Groups of employes were everywhere—on the street-corners, in front of tenements and boarding-houses, in the middle of the street;—and all were engaged in absorbing discussion of one exciting theme—the strike.

Men without coats or hats; women with shawls thrown loosely over their heads; girls, bonnetless and neglectful of dress; unkempt old women, who were perhaps the home-makers for these hard-worked and ill-paid people; all were indifferent save to one subject.

Even the quick passage, through their midst, of the pony-phaeton and its mistress failed to attract attention beyond. an occasional surly glance from the men or an envious one from the women. Unmindful of the long days in store, when there would be ample time to discuss their wrongs, they remained huddled in excited groups in the wet October air, talking over the strike,—the famous strike of the Shawsheen Mills.

"I declare!" muttered the young woman who was hurrying the pony out of these disagreeable surroundings; "it must be a strike! Nothing else would crowd them into the street so. I wonder what they want? Dear me! what nuisances these work-people are. Why can't they be sensible, and when they are earning a living, be content? Dear me! if I had the making over of this world I would make everybody comfortably off, and nobody rich— unless it were myself," she added, laughing; for absolute truthfulness was a necessity of Salome Shepard's nature, and she knew perfectly well that she could not do without the luxuries to which she had always been accustomed.

" If I had the making over of the world ! "

The words repeated themselves in her mind. If any human being has the power of making over the world in any smallest degree, something whispered, that person must be a young, attractive woman, with a vast property and absolute control of several hundred people, besides two millions of dollars in her own right.

"Dear me ! " she said aloud, as she drove up the graveled road under the dripping yellow beeches. " How positively dreadful it must be to be a reformer ! How would I look in a bloomer costume and black bombazine bonnet? No. Let things alone, keep to your sphere, young woman,—the proper, well-regulated, protected and chaperoned sphere of a delicate young lady, and let the world right its own wrongs."

She jumped lightly from the phaeton, tossing the reins to James, and showing her fine, well-turned figure to excellent advantage as she ran up the broad steps.

The massive doors turned noiselessly at her approach. She passed through the fine old hall and went directly up the broad oak staircase to her room.

"How comfortable this is," she said to herself, as the blazing wood-fire threw flickering shadows over the dainty hangings, the warm rugs and the choice pictures.

But even as she drew a long sigh of contentment with her lot, a picture of wet and muddy streets, thickset with groups of brawny men and bedraggled, unkempt women, intruded itself, and the sigh changed its tenor.

"If I only had the making over of the world!" she said again aloud; and added resolutely, "but I haven't."

II.

THE Shawsheen Mills had been established many years before the opening of this story by Salome's grandfather, Newbern Shepard. They constituted one of the chief manufacturing concerns of Shepardtown. They made more cloth, and that of a better quality, than any other mill outside the " City of Spindles." They employed a much larger force of operatives than any other factory in the place, and had always held a controlling interest in town affairs.

When the Shawsheen Mills were first started, blooming girls from all parts of Massachusetts came swarming to them, glad of a new and respectable employment,—came with earnest purpose to make this new life and its outcomes subservient to a better future. The conscientious New England girl of those days took as much pride in making a perfect web of cloth as though it were for her own wearing. Aware that her employers took an interest in her welfare, aside from the fact that she was a part of the motive power of the mill, she rewarded them with a full performance of her duty. A mutual goodfellowship had existed, then, between employer and employed in the years when old Newbern Shepard was at the head of his mills.

All this had changed. Newbern Shepard had died after a long and successful career, leaving the business to his son, Floyd Shepard. The latter, educated at Harvard, with five years of study afterward in Germany, had developed little taste for an active business life such as his father had led. He had, consequently, placed the entire business in the hands of Otis Greenough, a friend of his college-days and a hard-headed business man. Floyd Shepard had idled the greater part of his time before reaching the age of fifty in various parts of the world.

Then he came home, married a Baltimore belle, and passed his old age in his native place.

Even then, he gave little thought to the details of business. He added to and improved the home of his forefathers, until his house and grounds were acknowledged to be the finest in the state. After four years of married life, his young wife died, leaving him one child —a babe of three days. Then he retired into his study, and lived only among his books.

"Don't trouble me with the business," he would say to Otis Greenough, on the rare occasions when it seemed necessary to consult the owner of the mills. "I care nothing as to how you manage the works, and know less how it should be done. Suit yourself as to details, and keep the mills paying a good profit. I shall be satisfied."

Upon this principle the mills had been run for thirty years. The agent and his superintendents had devoted themselves to the problem of getting out more goods and making more money than their competitors, while keeping the standard of their wares up to its old mark. They had no time for the problem of human life involved. The first and principal question had required a severe struggle, with active brains and sharp wits. What wonder, then, that the increasing mass of operatives had come to be considered, every year, less as human beings in need of help and encouragement, and more as mechanical attachments of the mills?

Only such operatives as had been brought up in the mills realized the difference. The employes were mostly of the unwashed population, expecting nothing but a place to earn their living and but scanty pay for it.

Having, at the outset, no confidence in their employers, and no feeling of goodwill towards them, they had no conscientious motive behind their work. On the contrary, they stood on the defensive, watching for oppression and tyranny, and ready to take arms against them.

This was the state of things when the first regularly organized strike occurred at the Shawsheen Mills.

Otis Greenough, although an old man, was still at the head of the mills. Floyd Shepard's death three years before had made no difference with the vast business interests in his name. In willing everything he owned to his daughter, who was already heiress to a large fortune from her mother's family, he had provided that

Otis Greenough should be chief agent during the remainder of his life; and that the mills should continue on the same plan by which they had been run for the past quarter of a century.

Otis Greenough was an arbitrary man, with that enormous strength of will which a man must have who is to control and manage two thousand people and an increasing business.

If, in the march of economic progress, he chose to make changes in the machinery of the mills, he consulted no one, and cared nothing for the black looks or surly mutterings of the operative who might fancy himself injured thereby. Had it been hinted to him that his operatives might be trained to take a personal interest in the success or failure of new experiments or, indeed, that they had any right to his brotherly consideration, he would have flouted the idea.

It was his boast that he never wasted words on the operatives. In short, he was as indifferent to the rights of Labor as his Lancashire spinners were to the interests of Capital. Hence the strike.

At noon of the day that Salome Shepard

had driven through the factory street, Otis Greenough sat in his private office with his two superintendents, the treasurer and cashier of the mills, and one or two subordinates. As the bell struck for twelve, five men from the various departments filed in and presented a written document. They were the committee appointed by the new Labor Union.

Mr. Greenough took the paper with an air that showed him to be in anything but a conciliatory mood. Without opening it, he burst forth angrily :

"What, in the name of common-sense, is this farce anyhow? What do you mean by leaving your work and presuming to come here, dictating terms to *me* ?"

"The paper will explain everything, sir," replied the foremost of the committee. "We have our rights—or should have them. The time has come when we propose to get them. Will you read the petition, sir ?"

"No," thundered the choleric old man. "Not in your presence. Villard, treat with them." Mr. Greenough was too angry to say more.

Mr. Villard, the younger superintendent, stepped forward.

"I think," he said, "that you had better leave us for a time. We shall need to consider your proposals, whatever they may be. Go now, and come again later—say at four o'clock." Agreeing to this proposition, the five men turned and left the office. Mr. Villard sat down again, waiting for the agent to speak.

"The confounded whelps!" ejaculated Mr. Greenough, as soon as he could find breath. "Open that paper, Villard—the impudent puppies!"

Without answering, John Villard tore open the envelope, and read the document aloud:

Whereas, we, the undersigned, believing that our interests demand an organization which shall promote and protect affairs relating to us as laboring men; and

Whereas, we have already organized and maintained such a society; it is now unanimously agreed that we insist upon the recognition of such a body by our employers, and upon their making certain concessions for the benefit of that body.

Whereas, there is a ten-hour system established in this state by law; we hereby *resolve* that we will refuse to work ten and a half or eleven hours a day as has been demanded of us.

Whereas, we believe the introduction of the new frames are detrimental to the interests of the mule-spinners; we *resolve* that they must be taken out, and the old mules replaced, with a written agreement that no more of the obnoxious machinery shall be added for, at least, five years.

Whereas, there has been an attempt made to reduce our wages, especially in the weaving department; we hereby *resolve* that we will submit to no curtailment of wages, and to

2

demand payment of all wages weekly, as is the custom in certain other mills in this state.

Trusting that these our petitions may be granted, our rights respected, and that harmonious relations will soon be established between us, we take pleasure in signing ourselves

"MEMBERS OF THE SHAWSHEEN LABOR UNION."

Before John Villard had finished reading the paper, Mr. Greenough had risen and was pacing the floor excitedly.

"Shocking!" he exclaimed, as Mr. Villard folded the paper and returned it to its envelope. "Preposterous! Do they think they can impose upon me with such a jumble of unreasoning nonsense as that? Labor Union, indeed! Why, the rascals act as if there were no interests but those of labor. And a beautiful time they've taken to strike—when orders are pouring in faster than we can possibly keep up with them. A fine time, indeed!"

"I suppose," said John Villard, fearlessly, "there seems a slight injustice to them, in cutting down their wages at such a time."

"What right have they to dictate, I should like to inquire?" answered the irate agent. "If they were not a bigoted, unreasoning set, they'd know they never can serve the interests of labor in such a way. They'd realize that

they are only biting off their own noses ! They
have probably been worked upon by some
crank of an agitator. If they were not ignorant dogs, they'd know that they could best
serve the interests of labor by being faithful to
those of capital. Why," he concluded, his
face growing redder in his wrath, "is this
America ? Is this our boasted New England ?
Is this a free country ? By Jove ! I've heard
of this sort of thing in England, but in this
republican land, this boasted region of freedom—Great Scott ! What are we coming to ? "

"It's this accursed trades-unionism creeping
in among us," put in the treasurer's mild voice,
as Otis Greenough paused for breath. "I've
been expecting it."

"Blast it, why didn't you mention it then ? "
returned Mr. Greenough. But the treasurer
retired in confusion behind his books and did
not answer.

"Well, Villard," continued the agent, "I
hope now you will give up the Utopian schemes
you've been nursing for the elevation of the
laboring classes. You see just what a foolish,
unthinking, unreliable set of men we have to
deal with."

"On the contrary, sir," returned the second superintendent, firmly, "I sympathize, to a degree, with them. I agree that they have taken an inopportune time to enforce their views, and regret that they could not have seen fit to keep at work while their petition was being considered; and I would advise——"

"I want no man's advice until I ask it," interrupted the elder man. "This is our first strike, and it shall be the last so long as I have authority here. Humph! They think they can intimidate me! They have chosen this time because they think I *must* yield now. They little know me. Otis Greenough has not run the Shawsheen Mills successfully thirty years, to be brow-beaten and conquered in the end by a pack of ignorant laborers."

"But how is this to end?" asked the first superintendent, speaking for the first time.

"It can end whenever these men will take back their impudent paper and go to work. Villard, when they show up again—four o'clock did you say?—you will tell them so. Offer them a chance to go to work to-morrow morning on the old terms. You needn't give in to them one inch. Do you hear? Not a jot or tittle."

"And what if they do not accept?" asked Villard.

"Why, advertise. Advertise far and near. Get new help. We'll open the mills and run them, too, right in their very teeth. I'll show them that he who has been master here for thirty years is master until he dies."

III.

THE choleric agent's blood was fairly up, and he now set himself to plan for the coming warfare. When the committee from the labor union made its appearance at four o'clock, the agent refused to treat directly with them. He retired to his inner office, whence issued a moment later an " open letter to the employes of the Shawsheen Mills." The circular was composed and written entirely by himself, and was quite characteristic of his high-handed authority. It stated that " as the control of an owner over his property was guaranteed by the law of the land, and was of such unquestionable character as ought not to be meddled with by any other individual or combination of individuals, the agent of the Shawsheen Mills, acting for their owner, would brook no such interference as had been attempted."

But, in bombastic language, he went on to say that, on account of the pressure of work, he offered to take back into the mills such operatives as, after a day's idleness and a night's calm reflection, might decide to come back peacefully, and accept the old conditions. The circular closed by adding that all returning operatives must renounce their connection with the new Labor Union, and stating that the Shawsheen Mills would be immediately reopened.

This letter, as might have been expected, only served to fan the smouldering embers of discord. It was taken at once to the quarters of the new Union, and angrily discussed. A stormy meeting was held that evening, and scores of new members were added to the organization, all unanimously agreeing, not only to keep away from the mills themselves, but to prevent other operatives from entering them. The trouble which might have been met at the outset and subdued by candid discussion and a fair acknowledgment on each side of the claims of the other, was changed into a barricade of danger between labor and capital over which a battle was to be fought, involving money and credit and losses on one side, and daily bread for two thousand people on the other.

"Come," said Otis Greenough, emerging from his "den" after the committee had left the office. "I want you, Villard, and you, too, Burnham," he added, turning to the other superintendent, "to go with me this evening, to the owner of these mills, and lay before her the proceedings of the day, and our reasons for taking a firm stand. Although, precious little difference it will make with her, I imagine, how many strikes we have, until her income is affected! Will you be so good as to state, Villard, what you are smiling at."

"I was thinking, sir, that it is a queer state of affairs, when a person owning large and influential mills like these, need not know of the strike or be consulted with regard to it, until it is half over," answered Villard. He had no fear of the agent, with whom he was a favorite, in spite of his seeming harshness. "It seems to me, if I were a young woman, with unlimited leisure and wealth, I should care to know something of so tremendous an interest as the Shawsheen Mills represent—that is, if I owned them."

" Ha, ha!" laughed the agent, " that shows how much of a ladies' man you are, John. Much you know about the things that interest and amuse the young ladies. By Jove! I should laugh to see the daughter of Floyd Shepard meddling with the details of the great business he left her. She could discuss French and Italian literature, or the different schools of music and art, by the hour, and fairly inundate you with a flood of learning; but when it comes to mills—why, she don't know a loom from a spinning-jenny—and don't want to. I'm only going up there as a matter of form. As for advice, she knows I wouldn't take it, even if she has any to offer. But courtesy— proper courtesy," and Otis Greenough drew himself up to his fullest height, " and the respect we owe her as the owner of this property, demand that we go there this evening. I will call for you in my carriage at half-past seven." ·

And, so saying, he left the office.

" I reckon the old man is about right," said Burnham, when they were alone. " Miss Shepard knows no more about the practical affairs of her mill, than that little white kitten over there does. She'll meet us with a listless, half-bored air, pretending to listen to the statements of our chief, and all the time be wishing us at the antipodes."

"Do you know," interrupted John Villard, locking the door to the office as they left it together, "I've very little patience with women of that sort. Think, with her youth and health and money, what a directing, reforming force in bringing together the conflicting interests of labor and capital she might be! Great Heavens! I wish I had her opportunity. I'd make something of it."

"Oh, you are too Utopian," replied Burnham. "It is fortunate she isn't that kind. We should be overwhelmed with Schemes for the Amelioration of the Condition of This, That, and The Other Thing, until there would be nothing left but bankruptcy for all of us. No. I want no reformers in petticoats at the head of the Shawsheen Mills. But here I am at my street. Good-bye, till evening."

Salome Shepard passed a dull afternoon. Although a young woman of resources she found herself in no mood to enjoy any of them after lunch. The newest volume of essays seemed insufferably dull, and she turned for relief to the latest novel; but, in spite of the fact that this book was talked about throughout the country, she soon threw it aside with a wearied air and sat gazing into the blazing hickory fire.

Strange! but the red-hot coals formed themselves into a group against the dull back-log like the groups of miserable, excited men and women of the morning against a back-ground of rain and fog and muddy streets. It was an uncomfortable picture, and she rose suddenly, and, going into the music-room, seated herself at the piano. Chopin's Nocturnes stood open on the rack, but she tossed them aside and began some stormy Liszt music, breaking off when half done and going to the window.

The rain had begun to fall again and the fog had settled like a pall over everything farther off than the arched gateway. She wondered if all those people were still standing in the mud and rain.

An elderly lady, with soft white hair and exquisite laces, came in.

Salome ran forward, pushed her aunt's favorite chair into the position she liked best, and put her into it.

"Why did you stop playing? And why did you attempt that brilliant thing?" said Mrs. Soule. "You are so dreadfully out of practice, you know."

"It wasn't that," answered the younger woman; "I'm not in the mood for playing anything. I doubt if I could get through with 'Bounding Billows' or the 'Fifteenth Amusement' to-day. Did you know, aunty, there is a strike down at the mills?"

"A strike! Mercy, who has struck?" responded the elder in shocked tones.

"Why, the operatives, of course. I don't know why, or anything about it. I have never shown any interest in the mills," she went on eagerly and half-apologetically, "but I should like to know what it is all about—why they did it—what they want, and all that. I should think Mr. Greenough would come up here."

"He will come as soon as he deems it proper." Mrs. Soule's voice was calmness and precision itself. "It is not nice for young ladies to mix themselves up in such common things."

"But, aunty," laughed Salome, "strikes are not common things here. We never had one before.   And I am not so very young a lady as to need the same careful guardianship I had when I was sixteen.   I am twenty-seven years old."

" There is no need of saying so upon all occasions, if you are, " replied her aunt with some asperity.   " A strike, like all things connected with, or originated by the ignorant laboring class, is common in the sense of being vulgar.   Any woman, young or old, brought up as delicately and carefully as you have been, demeans herself by connection with such things.   You have an agent—a manly and capable one ; leave the settlement of such things to him."

" Oh, I'm not going to meddle with the strike. The very suggestion that I would wish to have anything to do with settling the difficulty makes me laugh."

Salome rose and began to pace the room. " But sometimes, lately, aunty, it has occurred to me that a young woman of average talent, with a great business on her hands which employs two thousand people, may have something to do in life more than to seek her own selfish enjoyment—a pursuit which, after all,

is not elevating and leaves but a restless, un-
satisfied spirit in its wake. I came across
some of grandfather's manuscripts two or three
weeks ago and have been reading them. He
wasn't like papa. The mills were a part of his
very self. The operatives were almost like so
many children to him. I've read in his, and in
other books, about the mill-girls of his day.
Girls whose working days began at daylight in
winter and ended at half-past seven in the
evening; who had only two dresses to their
backs, and those of Merrimack print; whose
profits for a week, after their board was paid,
were only two dollars. But girls who could
discuss Shakespeare, Dante, and Milton at their
looms; who read Locke and Abercrombie and
Pollock and Young (something I can't do!);
who sent petitions to Congress for the abolition
of slavery; who helped build churches from
their pitiful savings; who wrote essays and
poems and stories, even while running their
looms; who spent their evenings in the study
of German and French and botany; and
who went out, at last, to become teachers and
mothers and missionaries, and, above all, noble,
self-sacrificing, helpful women. And I tell you

that, with all my money and my polished education, I envy them."

" Salome, really, you surprise me," exclaimed the excellent lady who was listening to her. " Calm yourself, my dear."

" Look at the girls in this mill—in my grand-father's mill to-day—in my mill," she went on. " Beings of bangs and bangles and cheap jewelry, of low aspirations, and correspond-ingly low morals ! They are not to blame for their penny-dreadful lives, because they know no better. They dream of nothing higher than their looms and their face-powder, and their cheap satins and false hair—why should they ? They see rich and educated women like us wrapped entirely in ourselves, each anxious to outshine the rest, and all seemingly lost in the mad race after fashionable attire. They do not know, poor things, that we ever think or talk of higher subjects. I tell you, I feel that I am, somehow, responsible for them. And yet, I don't know how to help them. My grand-father could, but I can't."

"I know nothing of such things," coldly replied her aunt. "It is not ladylike to fly into a passion over the fancied wrongs of a lower order of beings. I beg that you will recollect that you are the daughter of Cora Le Bourdillon and Floyd Shepard."

"And more than that," Salome whispered to herself as she sought the quiet of her own room, "I am afraid I am the grand-daughter of Newbern Shepard."

IV.

IT was nearly eight o'clock when carriage-
wheels were heard coming up the graveled
drive-way, and Otis Greenough and his associ-
ates were announced.　Salome and her aunt
were sitting in the music-room, and came forward at once; the former with an unmistakable
air of eagerness.

"Tell me about the strike, Mr. Greenough,"
she asked, before he had fairly seated himself.

"Oh, then, you'd heard of it, eh?" he asked.

"I saw something of it this morning, driving
through the town.　I could not help knowing
what it was.　But why did they do it?　What
do they want?"

"They did it," and Otis Greenough sat up
with a judicial air, "because they are rascally
dogs, and do not know when they are well off.
And they want?—well,—the earth—more pay,
3

shorter hours, and the Lord knows what besides."

" Well, and why shouldn't they have it ? "

The question fell like a bomb upon her surprised audience.

" To be sure, I know very little of these
things, practically, although I have taken the
prescribed doses of social economy in my read-
ings under Professor Townsend," she went on ;
" but it has occurred to me, within a few days,
that the laboring classes have very little control
over their own lives, and are not much more
than slaves to us who hold the reins of
power."

" Bless me ' " thought Otis Greenough, staring at her. If his office-door had suddenly
spoken, offering him officious counsel as to
his method of conducting the mills, he could
hardly have been more surprised. " Bless me !
No Floyd Shepard about her."

"If the operatives are poorly paid, and we
are making more money than ever before (I
think I understood you so the other day ?),"
the young woman was saying, " why shouldn't
their wages be raised ? It seems but fair, to
me."

"Much you know about it, little girl," Mr. Greenough found voice to say, addressing her as he used to in by-gone days, when she occasionally strayed into the mills and teased to be taken through them. "Much any young lady of the world can know of such matters. We would not have you turn from being your own charming self, and become a learned blue-stocking, or bloomered reformer; but there are many, many reasons which come between the questions of profit and loss, and the petty details of operatives' wages, which cannot be explained to you here and now. They were contented enough until some rascal or other, having become imbued with the spirit of these labor unions starting up all over the country, must needs organize one here. By Jove! I'll employ detectives and hunt out the disturbing elements and shut them up. I have offered every mother's son a chance to go back to work to-morrow morning, on condition that he drops this union business; but I am told to-night that not one of them will accept. Ignorant creatures! I'll show 'em what it means to fight a rich and strong concern like this, in the vain hope of bringing us to their terms."

"Meanwhile," it was Villard who spoke, "we are to go on resisting their combined ignorance and impatience, and perhaps worse elements, losing thousands of dollars in the warfare, are we?"

"Yes, rather than give in one inch to them," answered Mr. Greenough. "This is the first organized strike and must be made a warning to future disturbers. It's those confounded Englishmen trying to transplant their foreign ideas to American soil. If we give in to them now, we establish a bad precedent."

"I must confess," said Villard, "that I do not see it. I have seen several strikes, and know that generally both sides lose sight of reason, and determine to fight it out regardless of cost. I am afraid, with the course you propose to adopt, sir, that we shall go on until the losses on our side or the suffering and privation on theirs will become unbearable; and then one side or the other will be forced to yield. If it should be they, a smouldering resentment will be left, ready to break out anew at the first convenient season. If we, they will feel encouraged to try still more arbitrary measures in the future. Or if a compromise be effected, it will be one that might as well be made to-morrow."

" You talk well for a young man," admitted Mr. Greenough. " How did you come by your exceedingly humane and sympathetic views?"

" I began as an employe myself," answered Villard, " and I know how they feel to some extent. I know what it is to work at the lowest drudgery of a mill, and can imagine how it must seem to have no hope of ever rising to a higher position. Hard, unremitting toil, long hours with endless years of hopeless work in prospect, the lowest possible wages, a large and rapidly increasing family, with perhaps an aged parent or invalid wife to support—I tell you lots of those fellows have all that to bear, knowing the utter impossibility of ever saving anything, or of raising their own condition. I say, sir, looking at life from their standpoint, it's mighty hard."

" Well, well," put in Mr. Greenough, testily, " a great many of them want nothing better. They would not know what to do with a better chance for life, as you call it, if they had it."

" Simply put yourself in their place, sir," said Villard. " What if you were forty years

younger than you are, and condemned to a life
of toil at the looms, for instance, would you not
claim the right to combine with others of like
occupation and interests and ask for a better
chance? These men of ours have taken an
unreasonable way of asserting themselves, but
I think they are entitled to our respect, and
should be dealt with as men. An open, fair
discussion of the wage question or the ten-hour
law can result in nothing but good for both
sides."

"You are young," Mr. Greenough replied,
"and believe everything in this world can be
made to run exactly as you want it. When
you are older, you'll realize better the indifference and general mulishness of the world, and
of operatives in particular. I do not believe in
meeting and deferring to them as equals. They
are not worth our efforts, and so long as they
are under the influence of hot-headed devils
who pose as labor reformers, just so long we
are going to see trouble."

"If we were to make a fair compromise with
them," Mr. Burnham was speaking for the
first time, "and let them see that we, as
humane employers, have a greater desire for

their interest than any foreigner can have,
wouldn't it work a reaction in our favor? From
a strictly business point of view, perhaps it
would be money in our pockets."

"Yes," urged Villard, "if we were to show
ourselves willing to consider an intimate knowledge of their needs and thus prove ourselves
their best friends, it would be only a case of
practical philanthropy, and one which would
raise our profits every year, I believe. It is
only the first step that costs, you know."

"I don't believe it," stoutly maintained the
agent. "In my day there has been very little
talk of managers and owners deferring to their
help. I hire my own operatives and reserve the
right to raise, or lower, their wages as I please."

"But, Mr. Greenough," broke in Salome
eagerly, "don't you consider their circumstances
at all? Don't you, for instance, in a driving
time, pay them any higher wages than in dull
times? I think there would be nothing but
fairness in that."

"My dear young lady," was the answer in
patronizing tones, "don't bother your brains
with such things. You cannot understand
them. Why try?"

"Imagine our Salome posing as a philan-thropist or a social economist," interrupted Mrs. Soule's mellifluous tones. " We had a great laugh over the idea this afternoon."

Salome bit her lip and said nothing.

" I think," continued her aunt in the same smooth accents, " that we have talked business long enough. I am sure, Mr. Greenough, that Salome is, and will be perfectly satisfied with any course you may see fit to adopt with regard to the strikers. Women, you know, ladies at least, have no heads for business, and we, certainly," with an indescribable turn of voice on the " we "—"we, certainly, have had no training to fit us for reformers. And now shall we not have some music ? Salome, dear, will you play that delightful little suite of Moscowzki's that I like so well ? "

The young woman rose and, going to the piano, did as she was bid, although some-what mechanically. Then Mr. Greenough proposed a song from Mr. Burnham, who pos-sessed a fine baritone voice, and the evening wore away with music and light conversa-tion.

When the three men went home, the elder

was in fine spirits, in spite of having been
shocked and discomfited to an unusual degree,
by the unexpected disclosure of views which he
termed " strong-minded " on the part of the
fair owner of the Shawsheen Mills.

" If there should come to be hard times and
perhaps destitution among the operatives before
this difficulty is settled," Salome said to John
Villard as he was preparing to go, " such destitution as we read of in foreign countries in
times of labor disturbances, I hope you will
let me do something to relieve it. Strange as
it may seem, I have a much better idea of
such a state of affairs there than here—among
my own mills."

" There will be no such state of affairs, I
trust," was his reply, " as is pictured in Eng-
lish novels."

" You have guessed accurately as to the
sources of my information," she laughed.

He smiled too, and continued,

" Meanwhile, if we pursue the policy proposed," and he glanced at Mr. Greenough, who
was making gallant speeches to Mrs. Soule,
" you might keep a watchful eye on the help.
You could tell, you know, by the women, if they

came to absolute distress.   Of course, there is no knowing how long this thing may last."

"Me ! You look to me for such a thing," and it was hard to tell whether her tone was amused or sarcastic only.   "Why, Mr. Villard, I do not know one of the operatives in the mills— not even by sight.   If I were to meet them on the main thoroughfare to-morrow I should not know them from other women of their class."

John Villard raised his eyebrows and turned to put on his coat without another word.   The situation was incomprehensible to him.

Salome saw this, and winced under it.   She made no further attempt at conversation, but said good-night graciously to Mr. Greenough and the older superintendent, recognizing Villard's parting nod at the door.

" There," said her aunt, as they went back into the firelight, "I hope they won't feel it necessary to come here and consult with us again so long as the strike is on.   As though you knew or cared anything for it, my dear ! But, of course, they had to come as a matter of form.   Any way, I'm glad it is over.   Play something."

Salome complied, playing the first thing which came to her mind—the opening bars of the *Sonata Pathetique*.

"I wish," she said to herself as she. disrobed for the night, "that I were a capable woman of affairs—and that John Villard were my agent."

V.

Not for a week could enough new help be hired to even make a show of opening the Shawsheen Mills. Labor Unions were a comparatively new thing in this country, and were not so thoroughly organized as now ; and a few of the old operatives, rather than starve, were glad to go back into the mills on any condition. But the great majority refused with indignation to give up their claims, and proceeded to "make things hot," as they expressed it, for the "scabs" and "mudsills."

Work was attempted in the mills, although many looms stood silent and the spinning-mules were entirely deserted. Thread for warp was procured from a neighboring city at no small expense and the mills were run at a loss, to prove the agent's assertion that " he would show them who was manager of the Shawsheen Mills.".

This sort of thing was kept up four days. On the fifth morning, the operatives went as usual to the mill, but the machinery, after a few insufficient groans, gave up in despair and settled into utter quiet.

What was the matter?

There was a great hurrying to and fro, and a close examination of belts and machinery. Word was soon brought up from the basement. The engines had been tampered with; on each of them the belts had been cut. The jocularly inclined said the " engines had joined the Union ; " — while everybody wondered what effect this stroke would have on the agent.

The premises were examined and the night-watchman questioned. Evidently the deed had been done by some one familiar with the place, but there was not the slightest clue. He had done well his work, and the mills were stopped for repairs.

Otis Greenough blustered about and cursed the whole business ; but he was farther than ever from a compromise, declaring that he would yet beat them with their own weapons.

The night-watch was doubled and the mills
were opened again the next day.   But the employers were fighting a desperate party and little
calculated their strength.   The man who had
succeeded so well in his first attempt to stop the
mills risked himself again ; and on the second
morning the machinery again refused to start.
This time a small wheel had been removed
from each   engine and carried away.   The
water-wheel had long been in partial disuse and
could not be trusted without the engines.
Hence, there was nothing to be done but to stop
again for repairs.   This time it was a week
before the engines were in running order.
And yet, not a word passed between the agent
and the strikers.

The night-watch were discharged and new
ones engaged.   A special police was secured to
patrol the mill-yard, and when the mills were
again opened, it was with the avowed determination to keep them going in spite of every
earthly power.

The   next morning, notwithstanding   the
positive assertions of police and night-watch
that no one had been near the mills, every
band connecting the looms to the machinery

above was cut in half a dozen places. Then
the superstitious operatives whispered among
themselves that unseen agencies were linked
with the Union, and that the strikers must
succeed in the end; and many of the faint-
hearted went over to the new labor party.

"It is of no use trying to run the mills in this
way," said Mr. Burnham. "We have already
lost several thousand dollars. We must compromise."

"Never," said Mr. Greenough. "The terms
of Floyd Shepard's will grant me absolute
power here, and so long as I live, it shall never
be said that an educated, trained and level-
headed business-man was overcome by a lot
of ignorant bullies and agitators. These Labor
Unions all over the State need an example.
There is money enough in the mill treasury to
fight them until they starve themselves out.
No other mill or corporation about here will
hire them, and it is only a matter of weeks
or months when absolute poverty forces them
to yield. Not one inch will I give in to them.
They shall come back as beggars, glad to
accept work at even lower wages than they
have ever had. I'll teach them a lesson."

Geoffrey Burnham turned away full of anger that a flourishing business should be destroyed by one man's obstinacy. John Villard went back to the silent looms, full of righteous indignation, not only at the total disregard of practical business interests, but at the want of humanity and philanthropy and Christian charity, which by his subordinate position he must seem to countenance.

Weeks lengthened themselves into months, and still the Shawsheen Mills were closed.

Salome Shepard, after spending the holiday season with friends in New York, came home, satiated with social success, and a little tired of the endless pursuit of pleasure. Still the mills lay idle and Otis Greenough refused to talk any more with her on the subject of the strike. And the terms of her father's will held her powerless, even had she chosen to exercise her authority.

But she chafed under the knowledge that two thousand people, who were in a sense dependent upon her for their daily bread, were out of work in the midst of a hard winter.

One day she went to walk down among the people who were suffering, now, for a principle.

She was amazed at the gaunt, hungry look
of the old men ; and self-accused at the
pinched and wan faces of the few children who
played in the narrow streets. Unthinking, she
had put on a seal-skin cloak. It was a cold
day, and furs, to her, were only a natural
accompaniment to the frosts of winter.

But going down the uncared-for side-walk,
she rebuked herself, noting the single shawl
and calico dress of an old woman who was
wearily making her way a few paces in front
of her. Presently the woman stopped, seized
with a paroxysm of coughing.

Salome came up with her, and looked into
the white face, which told of hard times.

" Madam," she said, respectfully, " can I be
of any assistance to you ? Shall I not help
you home ? "

Her tone and manner were exactly the same
she would have used to any of her aunt's
friends. It did not occur to her to be patronizing or condescending.

The old woman stared at her. She was not
used to being addressed as " Madam."

" Yes'm," she said, presently. " I live up
to the other end of the street. If the cough

4

wasn't so bad, an' my side didn't ketch me so ! But if I can git back to my own chair ag'in——"

Another fit of coughing seized her, and interrupted the " garrulousness of uncultured old age." Salome waited until she got breath again and then took her by the arm, accommodating her steps to the feebler ones.

Here and there a surprised face peered curiously at her through a dirty window, knowing who she was, and wondering that she condescended to walk with old Granny Lancaster. Everywhere a general air of poverty, perhaps of actual hunger, impressed this woman, who had inherited the tumble-down tenement houses on each side.

" I beg your pardon," she said, "but do you eat nourishing food enough ? Good beef-steak and roast-beef would help your cough more than medicine."

The old woman laughed, a grating, cackling laugh.

" Beef-steak and roast-beef ain't for the likes o' me," she said. " Meat of any kind ain't for us in times o' strikes. May the Lord above send us oatmeal enough to keep us through

till the mills open ag'in is all I ask. Here's my
house. Much 'bleeged, lady."

Salome wanted to go inside the rickety old
door and follow the woman up the dirty stairway, but she did not say so, and the old woman
hobbled up the steps without asking her in.

Salome felt impulsively in her pocket, and
drawing out her porte-monnaie, emptied its
contents into the dirty, emaciated palm of
Granny Lancaster. Then she turned and
walked rapidly back home.

The next day Otis Greenough called on her.

"My dear," he said, after an hour or two
passed in desultory conversation, "may I beg
that you will keep away from the operatives ?
Impulsive and injudicious charity does them
more harm than anything else. No doubt the
part of Lady Bountiful seems a pleasant and
desirable one, but, just now, you are not fitted
for it."

"What do you mean, sir?" asked she in a
puzzled tone.

"For instance," he went on, "the money
you gave a certain old woman on the corporation yesterday was taken by her son-in-
law last night, and furnished him an opportu-

nity for a glorious old drunk. I beg your
pardon for using their phraseology. He was
arrested before morning for drunkenness and
disorderly conduct."

"I do not comprehend," she stammered.
"The woman said they had no meat. She was
actually suffering for nourishing food. I gave
the money, impulsively it is true, but that
they need not go hungry."

"Now, you see, my dear," he answered,
"just how much encouragement one gets in
trying to do anything for the laboring classes.
They turn upon you and use the goodness of
your heart and your generous motives to drag
themselves down to a lower depth of degradation. Good-day, my dear, and don't be led
away by your feelings."

Salome stood looking after him, heart-sick
and discouraged. The world—her part of it,
at least—was all wrong, and she, with plenty
of money and an awakening desire to help, was
powerless. She ordered the pony phaeton
again and started for a drive. She obeyed a
sudden impulse to go through the factory precincts. There were evidences of a suppressed
excitement. Knots of desperate-looking men

stood about. But they hushed their voices as she drew near, and stood in sullen silence as she passed.

"There is evidently something in the wind," she thought, urging the pony to quicken his pace.

She did not know that the committee from the Labor Union had that morning made a third attempt to treat with her agent and failed.

"No compromise," was still his watchword.

"I'll send for Marion Shaw," she said to herself, on her way home an hour later. "She is a practical, sensible, business-like woman. Perhaps she will know of some way to help me to help others. And she needs rest."

This idea so inspired her that she arrived home quite elated, and stated her plan to Mrs. Soule at dinner-time with much animation.

But later in the evening, the groups of men she had seen on "the corporation" came back to her mind and caused her a certain feeling of uneasiness. What had they been talking about so excitedly as she drew near?

It was one of those suddenly warm nights in January that succeed, in our fickle climate, a bitter cold day, and Salome felt an unaccountable desire to be in the open air. She threw on a warm wrap and hood, and saying nothing, went out on the piazza, and crossed the lawn to a favorite walk of hers in summer—a path under a long group of fir-trees down by the street at the back of the house.

After a few turns, she heard a peculiar whistle which was answered by another.

She withdrew still more into the shadow and waited. Presently two men met.

"Well, what's the news?" eagerly asked one.

"Sh—sh! not so loud," replied the other. "It's all right, and better than we expected."

"Why—how better?" asked the first.

They spoke lower, so that Salome could scarcely catch the tones.

"Because," the first was saying, "the old man himself has gone down to the mill."

"Whe—e—w!"

"Yes. What on earth possessed him? But then that's none of our affairs. If he wants to run the risk of losing his life—that's his business, not mine."

"Well, but," and the first voice had a timid

note, " that's going too far—we were only to blow up the mill—not to kill anybody."

" Can't help that. Fifteen minutes more, if everything works well, and old man Greenough's day is over. Jim's just about lighting the fuse, I reckon, now. It's an awful long one, but the fire'll creep round there in time."

" What about the police ? "

" He's all right. We've fixed him."

The voices grew fainter and ceased altogether, only the dull sound of the men's footsteps reaching her as they passed down the hill away from the grounds.

Salome stood an instant, rooted to the spot. What was this horrible thing she had heard ?

The factory to be blown up ?

She must go for help.

And Mr. Greenough down there, risking his life ?

No. There was no time to get help.

" Fifteen minutes more, if everything works well, and old man Greenough's day is over."

The whole plot flashed across her bewildered brain. She dashed through the back-gate and down the deserted street towards the mills. It was a ten minutes' walk across that way, but she ran,—flew,—tore down the lonely road in less than half that time.

Otis Greenough might be an unreasonable, hot-headed, obstinate agent, but he was her father's friend and had loved and petted her when she was a motherless child.

What could she do? Raise an alarm? Call for help? Rouse everybody?

But the fuse was already lighted.

Where was it?

Under the office window most likely, since they knew that the old agent was in there.

She came in sight of that window. There was a dim light there. All else was dark. The south wind moaned dismally.

She hurried faster and came nearer the office window. Under it was another window with a broken pane, from which hung something she instantly divined as the fuse.

Yes. A fiery spark crept closer and closer to the wall.

By the time she reached the window it was out of her reach.

Oh, God! could she do nothing?

She had been sewing on some dainty trifle

earlier in the evening, and a pair of small scissors still hung at her waist.

Closer drew the spark of fire to the broken window pane, whence it would disappear to work its fearful errand. It seemed to twinkle and mock at her in fiendish delight. She grasped the jutting window-frame and jumped upon the broad sill.

Thank God, she had it at last. One snip of her scissors, and the spark of fire dropped harmlessly to the ground. She turned slightly to step off the window-ledge. Her foot slipped and she fell, a white, faint heap upon the ground.

VI.

WHEN she opened her eyes again, not only
Otis Greenough but John Villard and an office-
boy were bending anxiously over her.

" My dear girl," the agent was saying, " bless
me, my dear, what is it ? How came you here
and who has harmed you ? "

" Don't be alarmed, sir," was her reply, as
she got on her feet; and then, somewhat
excitedly, she told the events of the last fifteen
or twenty minutes, interrupted, every other
sentence, by such ejaculations as, " Great Scott,"
" Bless me," " The rascals," " Confound them,"
from the elderly man, while the younger one
listened in silent amazement.

Rapid search was made and the night-watch
was found sleeping, in a stupor which was evidently the work of a drug ; while the police
were, as usual, nowhere to be found.

Salome was taken into the office—not without inward trembling, as she feared further evidences of the miscreants.

Mr. Villard soon reported two kegs of gunpowder and a small dynamite bomb in the room below, at the same time congratulating, most heartily, the young woman who had saved their lives as well as the mills.

But her courage was now at a low ebb, and, woman-like, she shivered at the close proximity of gunpowder, and begged to be taken home.

Mr. Greenough, who had come to realize the danger to himself and to the mills which his obstinacy had provoked, was also anxious to leave the premises and glad to accompany Salome home.

John Villard, meanwhile, attended to the duty of finding new watchmen who should be reliable,—a difficult task. Against his will, he promised Salome not to sleep at the mills, as he had been doing since the machinery had been tampered with.

Salome was nearly prostrated when she reached home, and had but little strength left with which to importune the agent to consent to any terms for a settlement; but as the old man was, for once, thoroughly frightened, it was not difficult to exact a promise that he would consider a compromise.

Mrs. Soule, when she learned of Salome's intrepidity,—set forth as it was by Mr. Greenough's gratitude and gallant appreciation,—was greatly concerned for her niece and put her straightway to bed, where, in fact, she had supposed her to be for the past hour, and where she wept over and caressed her as she had not done since the girl had left home for boarding-school. And then, what was far more to the purpose, she gave her a bath of alcohol and olive oil, and soothed her to sleep.

Early the next morning the agent of the Shawsheen Mills sent a messenger over to the dingy room which served as headquarters for the Labor Union, begging for an interview.

As this was the first overture of peace from his side, it was natural that it should be hailed with glee by the officers of the Union. And although, the day before, the leaders of the strike had been closeted together in a serious debate as to how much they should yield to Capital, they now unanimously agreed not to "weaken" in the smallest degree.

As for the agent, he had been persuaded to
yield every point demanded by the strikers, insisting only upon the one condition, that the
Labor Union should be disbanded.

The question of ten hours he granted without a murmur. He quibbled a long time over
the wage-question, and the subject of weekly
payments, and only on seeing the dogged determination of the laborers did he come to terms
on that. But he very properly, and too
peremptorily, refused to remove the spin-
ning frames which had formed one subject
of contention. And then he proceeded to
overthrow the good effects of what concessions he had made, by violently denouncing all
labor unions, and vigorously insisting that the
one known as the Shawsheen Labor Union be
immediately and forever disbanded.

" Never," said the foremost of the committee,
" will we submit to so arbitrary a demand. We
have a perfect right to organize our forces and
assert our claims. How can we—a band of
day-laborers,—dependent on capital for a bare
living, win a single cause for ourselves without
combinations of this kind ? There are scores of
questions which involve not our welfare in one

way alone, but our health, our wages, our
morals, our manhood, which we, as single individuals, can never cope with, but which, as a
united force, we can adjust. Besides, in all
departments of labor, the women and children
equal or exceed the men. There are to-day
one hundred and seventy-five thousand more
women working in mills than there were ten
years ago; and what are they but the weakest
and most dependent of employes? They have
no strength to agitate; they have no power to
change any existing order of things. All they
can do is to toil and submit. We owe it to
them as men, as husbands, brothers, and sons,
to lighten their burdens. As free American
citizens we owe it to ourselves, to settle the
conditions of our own lives, so far as may be.
This can only be done by combinations of the
laboring classes strong enough to compel manu-
facturers to concede us our rights."

" You are right to a degree," answered Villard, before Mr. Greenough could swallow his
surprise at hearing such sentiments from one of
his operatives; " I believe there are some rights
which you can only secure by a combination of
your forces as working-men. But when you

let reason lose its sway, and passion take its place ; when you are influenced by unworthy demagogues and unbalanced cranks, and seek to effect by strikes and such arbitrary measures what might be better secured by a more con- ciliatory course, you must not be surprised if you do not succeed in bull-dozing a rich con- cern like this into obedience, and——"

" And when, by your —— labor unions, you sink so low as to countenance incendiarism and murder—yes, sirs—that is what you attempted last night, sirs,—you can't expect this mill is going to countenance them. I'll see you all starve and rot first," and Otis Greenough's face was purple with anger.

" We have already disclaimed all knowledge in our Union, sir," said one of the committee, " of last night's outrage."

" Blast it, what do I care for that ? " roared the agent, as usual, out of temper. " Whether you knew it or not, it was done under cover of your strike, and your Union, and was one of the precious outgrowths of it. Give up the —— thing, I say—or there is no compromise with these mills."

" There is little use in prolonging this interview, I am afraid," said the first of the committee, taking up his hat.

"Impudent dogs!" said Mr. Greenough, as Villard tried to speak, anxious to put things on a more satisfactory basis before the meeting closed. "Let them go. They'll find hard hoeing before they reach the end of their row."

"And, sir," retorted a fiery-looking man who had not spoken before, "if it comes to open war you'll find us tough customers. We shall fight it out like men, even if we starve like beasts."

And with these words the committee departed, leaving matters worse than ever before in the affairs of the Shawsheen Mills.

In vain did the two superintendents plead and argue and threaten the choleric old agent. His blood was up and he was a veritable charger on the eve of battle. There was no state board of arbitration then, and therefore no available way of settling their difficulties except among themselves. And as discussion only made matters worse, the subject which was always uppermost in these three men's minds was tacitly dropped. Every precaution was taken to insure the mills from the danger it had escaped the night before, and a detective was obtained from Boston to hunt out the criminals who had perpetrated the dastardly act.

At noon, they were all surprised by a note from Miss Shepard. It ran as follows:

"DEAR MR. GREENOUGH,

"As the owner of the Shawsheen Mill property, I hereby appoint a meeting of all its officers at my house, to-night. Please have them here at eight o'clock.

"Pardon me for the liberty I have seemed to take, and believe me ever a loving and respectful friend,

"SALOME SHEPARD."

"Well, you hear that, boys," said Mr. Greenough, after reading it aloud. "Be on hand. Tell the treasurer and cashier and head book-keeper. We'll all be there. The Lord only knows what she is up to; but if that young woman hasn't got a level head on her shoulders, then I don't know who has."

"I reckon you're right, sir," echoed Mr. Burnham, while John Villard laughed in his sleeve at the young woman who evidently dreamed of settling a prolonged strike. "Why," he said to himself, "she has never known enough of the practical side of mill-life to recognize one of her operatives, and hardly knows the different brands of cloth manufactured by them."

* * * * *

Salome Shepard had waked at an early hour that morning and found herself unable to sleep again. Her mind was alive with gratitude for the part she had been able to play the night before, with apprehension for the future, and with increasing self-accusation for the state of things in the Shawsheen Mills, both past and present.

"Pshaw!" she said to herself while dressing, true to her habit of communing with her own conscience in default of a visible mentor, "how can I be blamed for the state of things here? The entire business of the mills was put out of my hands by my father's will. I could have done no differently."

"You could," replied that sternest of modern inquisitors—a New England conscience. "It was in your power to see that the moral and physical condition of these people was improved and cultivated. It was in your power to give them better homes and more privileges. It was in your power to raise their standards of life and to create new ones. But you have ignored their very existence, and let them live a mean and sordid life of unremitting toil, in order to furnish you with money to live a selfish life of luxurious ease."

Salome tied the blue ribbons to her wrapper, and giving her crimps a last touch went down to breakfast.

Knowing she would be opposed, she said nothing of her plans for the morning to her aunt, but simply announced, after they had left the table, that she was going for a long walk.

Then she went upstairs and put on the plainest costume she owned (which, by the way, was a tailor-made gown that had cost her one hundred and fifty dollars), and started for the tenement houses where her operatives lived.

It did not occur to her to feel any fear ; nor that the miscreants who had planned the explosion for the previous night might be watching her footsteps. She felt it incumbent upon her to see for herself exactly how these people lived, and what they were bearing and suffering in consequence of the strike.

In the bright glare of the morning sun, the tenement houses had never looked so dingy and mean. They were built in Newbern Shepard's day, and had received but very few repairs since that time. Although it was cold January weather, Salome counted a dozen panes of glass gone from the first house, and noticed that the lower hinge to the front door was broken. It was a 'two-story wooden building with four tenements of four rooms each.

She ascended the rickety steps and rapped on the door. One of the women saw her from a front window and came to the door, holding it open only so far as to permit her to see the strange caller.

"Good-morning," said Salome in pleasant tones.

"Good-morning, miss." The politeness of Salome's manner thawed the other woman, and the door opened a little wider. "Will you walk in?"

That was precisely what she had come for, and Salome stepped inside with alacrity. She found herself in the sitting-room and living-

room of the family. It was a meager home.
The remnant of a faded oil-cloth was on the
floor. The walls were unpapered and devoid
of any attempts at ornament, except one un-
framed, dilapidated old lithograph of "The
Queen of the West,"—a buxom young woman
with disproportionately large black eyes, a
dress of bright scarlet cut extremely *décolleté*,
and cheeks of a yet more vivid hue. A pine
table covered with a stamped red cloth was
littered with cheap, trashy story-papers and
pamphlets addressed "To the Laboring Men
of America." An old lounge, with broken
springs, and six common wooden chairs constituted the other furnishings of the room.

Salome's first thought as she looked about
her was :

"I don't wonder these people get discontented and clamor for something which seems
to them better."

But she found, before the forenoon was over,
many houses that were not so pleasant as this.
For, once inside these rooms, everything was
neat and clean, and the woman who answered
her questions was civil if not talkative.

She found that five people lived in these

four small rooms: this woman, her two
daughters, a son-in-law, and a grandchild.
She also found that the other tenements contained five, six, and seven people, making
twenty-three in all. There were absolutely no
sanitary arrangements, and she discovered that
the sanitation of this tenement house district
consisted only of surface drainage. According to
the statements of her hostess, there was nearly
always somebody " ailing " in these houses.

The first house she went into was a fair
sample of the remainder. A few were slightly
better, but more were in a worse condition. In
most instances she was respectfully received,
although at three houses she was met by un-
gracious people, and received gruff replies to
her kindly-put inquiries.

Everywhere, strong, able-bodied men were
lounging about in enforced idleness; and one
of them, resenting, with true American inde-
pendence, this intrusion into the sacred precincts of his miserable home, plainly intimated
that " they was well enough off now, and didn't
want no rich folks as was livin' on money *they*
earned, to come pryin' round their houses."
Finally, at the last of the tenement houses she

was met by a surly, burly mule-spinner, who
gruffly refused her admittance.

Nothing daunted, however, she sought out a
boarding-house for the young women of the
mills. The landlady, recognizing her, invited
her in and willingly told her all about the life
of mill-girls, offering, at last, to show her their
rooms.

Salome gladly accepted and followed the
woman up bare, unpainted stairs to the rooms
on the second and third floors. These were
small and perfectly bare of comforts, almost of
necessities. The floors were uncarpeted and
guiltless of paint, or even of a very recent application of soap and water. They had no closets.
A common pine bedstead—sometimes two of
them—in each room, two chairs, in one of
which stood a tin basin, while beside it on the
floor stood a bucket of water, and a small
bureau, made up the sum total of the furniture.
In only one room did Salome see any evidences
of a literary taste, and that, if she had known
it, was a cheap paper, the worst of the sensa-
tional class.

Salome's heart sank within her. She no
longer wondered that the mill-girls of to-day

were a discontented, ignorant set, nor that
many of them sank into lives of degradation.

"The rooms are good enough for the girls,"
said the woman, noticing the look of disgust
on Salome's tell-tale face. "They seem poor
enough to elegant ladies like you. But these
girls know no better. And they are good
enough to sleep off a drunk in," she added,
roughly.

"You don't mean to say," asked her guest,
"that any of your girls get intoxicated?"

"Intoxicated? I don't know what else
you'd call it, when they have to be helped in
at eleven o'clock Saturday night, and put to
bed, and don't get up again until Monday
morning."

Salome was sick with pity and shame for
her sex. She no longer questioned whether
she had a mission toward these, her people.

She went home and wrote the note to Mr.
Greenough, given in an earlier part of this
chapter.

VII.

Promptly, at the hour named, Otis Greenough, accompanied by the other officers of the
mill, appeared at the mansion of the Shepard
family.

Tall, beautiful, and always impressive in her
bearing, Salome was at her best to-night.
The fire of a new-born purpose was in her
face, and a new force, born of spiritual strug-
gles, stamped upon her brow.

There are people who can look calmly upon
a sunset, and see nothing but a glare of red and
yellow light. There are others who see in it
a glorious picture with matchless tints and
shadows. There are yet others, fewer, indeed,
than the rest, but who hold the secret of God's
holy purpose written more or less plainly in
their souls; who see not only the glare of red
and yellow light, whose brilliant tints and deep

tones make an unrivaled picture, but who read something of the deeper meanings of the Great Artist; who receive into their own hearts some part of the glowing light which strengthens purpose, and crystallizes hopes and ideals hitherto dreamy and undefined.

Salome Shepard had stood at a western window at sunset. In the hush and stillness of the hour, the poet-quality of her soul had interpreted to her the meaning of life and the great fact of human brotherhood. And when she finally drew the curtains on the deepening night, she felt that a sudden revelation had come to her—that, at last, her life purpose, in the shape of a sternly defined duty, stood revealed.

"Well," said Mr. Greenough, after a few moments of aimless conversation, for nobody seemed desirous of taking the initiative, "what are you going to do with us all to-night, little girl? Don't you think you rather usurp the privileges of an old man in calling together a meeting to discuss business, of which he is the legal head? Come, give an account of yourself and your quixotic actions."

"Oh, I beg that none of you will think

that," And Salome looked around the room appealingly. " I simply wished that we might have a fair and honest talk. I want every one here to express his views. And I want to express mine—for at last, thank heaven, I have some."

" Getting strong-minded, eh ? " retorted Mr. Greenough. " Well, go on. I suppose you want to practice on us before taking a larger field. Going to take the suffrage platform? or build school-houses for the niggers? Or do you aspire to the bureau of Indian Affairs? Which is it? "

" None of them," responded Salome, inwardly resenting the untimely jest, but determined not to show her impatience. " None of them. I propose to begin nearer home. I propose to go to work, earnestly, and I hope practically, to raise the condition, morally, mentally and physically, of my own factory-people."

"Bravo ! " exclaimed Villard and the head book-keeper.

" And I have called you here," pursued Salome, " to ask each and every one of you to be my assistant and coadjutor. I have not been thinking of nothing, during the last three months. I am a woman, comparatively young, and with absolutely no knowledge of the practical side of a working-man's life. But I have been thinking, and my conclusions are these : that a strike is a much more serious matter for the working-people than it is for us. We act as if they go out on a strike either to annoy us or to have a good time. I have been down among them — sought the by-ways and hedges, as it were—and I tell you they are having anything but a good time. This strike is the outcome of want and privation, and it has brought the people to still greater want and privation. I believe they are not a set of noisy malcontents on the lookout for an opportunity to create a disturbance. On the contrary, they see in this course the only chance of bringing before the public questions of vital importance to them. They earn their bread by the sweat of their brow—and not always good bread either,—while we, as capitalists, are hoarding up money. At the most, they get very little of what their work really yields. I desire, above all things, sir, that you grant their desires and no longer require them to give up their Labor Union.

Capitalists have their Board of Trade, which virtually amounts to the same thing. Let the workmen have their one chance to assert themselves by a combination of their forces. And let each side show to the other that tolerance and Christian charity which each demands from the other."

"What about the tolerance and Christian charity of the outrage they tried to perpetrate last night?" asked Mr. Greenough.

"I do not believe the Labor Union is responsible for that," replied Salome, with a far-seeing sympathy in her eyes. "Unfortunately it was an outgrowth of their opinions, passions and prejudices. But you must confess, sir, that had you met them with the tolerance which the growing spirit of the age demands, there is little likelihood that matters would ever have reached the point where such an action could have been planned. I want this strike ended on any terms. I want to see the operatives, every one of them, at work again at fair wages. And then, God helping me, I propose to do something for their elevation—something to help them live better, cleaner, manly and womanly lives—something which shall carry out my grandfather's noble plans, and help make the factory system of New England one of her grandest achievements."

"Miss Shepard is right," said Mr. Burnham : "our factory, like many another, has been run too long on the system of *laissez-faire*. I have come to believe in a political economy which insists upon the liveliest activity on the part of capitalists, to put their employes upon the best possible footing as to the material surroundings of life ; that they have all the advantage as to health, morals and happiness which comes from sanitary regulation and practical education. I believe that only when we adopt such a political economy as this shall we draw the largest possible dividends from the products of a community comparatively free from crime, intemperance, poverty and vice of every kind."

"Yes," urged Villard, "each one of us, laborer or capitalist, has duties to perform which cannot be shirked or shifted to the shoulders of Fate—another name for the theory of *laissez-faire*. The new political economy will demand that every one who, in his or her public or private capacity, can do anything to relieve misery, to combat evil, to redress wrong,

to assert the right, shall do so with heart and
soul."

"You see," said Salome, delighted that two
strong, thinking men thus endorsed and voiced
her sentiments, "we have been acting on the
Quaker's advice to his son : 'Make money—
honestly if you can; but make money.' We
have forgotten that Christianity says : 'Thou
shalt love thy neighbor as thyself,' 'Do unto
others as ye would that men should do unto
you,' 'Bear one another's burdens,' and 'Love
one another.' But we have practically said :
'Love thyself; seek thine own advantage; promote thine own welfare; put money in thy purse;
the welfare of others is not thy business.'"

"I must confess," answered Otis Greenough,
speaking slowly and huskily, "that I cannot,
after a life-long devotion to old-fashioned ideas,
take any stock in these new-fangled, impracti-
cable ones. I cannot, at my time of life, change
my ideas; and neither can I endorse your proposition to make a public spectacle of ourselves
in the future. Mills are run to make money.
So long as I hold the position imposed upon
me by the late Floyd Shepard, so long shall
I refuse to countenance extravagance and quix-

otism. But I am an old man. No one cares any longer what I think. It is the young people with no experience whose opinions count nowadays. I am an old man who has had his day——"

" Don't, I beg of you, sir, talk like that," interrupted Salome. " We do value your opinion ; we do intend to refer to your judgment ; we——"

" What is that ? " cried Mrs. Soule in alarm, from her seat near the window.

" It is some one throwing gravel against the panes," said the cashier as a second shower came rattling against the window. He parted the curtains and looked out.

" The grounds are full of men. We are mobbed, by George ! "

The old agent's blood was up in a moment, and regardless of the presence of ladies he swore in good, set terms, that the rascals should be arrested and imprisoned for this.

Then, unconscious of danger, in spite of the attempts of Villard and the rest to hold him back, he marched, like an old hero, boldly out on to the veranda which faced a crowd of excited workmen.

They had held a stormy meeting at the Labor Union, and the worst element among them had become desperate, and swore to "bring the old man to terms." They had gone in a body to the mills, where they hoped to find some of their employers in consultation. There they had found that the whole force of their opponents had gone to the great Shepard Mansion. Nothing daunted, they turned their steps thither, and at every street corner were joined by the element of hoodlumism which is always scattered about over the streets of a large and poorly-governed town.

Hence the mob that confronted the officers of the Shawsheen Mills held all the elements of danger and disturbance.

When Otis Greenough's bald head appeared before them, the crowd set up a yell of mingled derision and defiance.

"Give us our rights, old Baldy" shouted one voice.

"Give us fair play and fair wages," called another, while worse epithets were hurled at him, from the roughs in the rear.

Otis Greenough's face was purple.

"This is outrageous!" he exclaimed in hot

6

haste. "What right have you to come here and defile an honest citizen's premises with your wretched, polluting presence?"

"Stop that, now!" shouted one of the leaders. "Fair play all round. If you won't come to us, we'll come to you, and compel you to make terms, and decent ones, with us. We want——"

But the crowd of street idlers who had come in search of excitement, and not argument, grew restless, and broke in noisily; and when Otis Greenough opened his mouth to speak again, he was struck squarely in the face by a handful of gravel and mud.

Then a sudden hush fell over the mob.

For what was this unexpected white form which appeared in the doorway, and advanced to meet them?

Salome was dressed in a clinging, white, soft serge, with falls of fine lace at the neck and wrists, and under the dim light of the piazza-lamp, she seemed like an angel of retribution, her eyes flaming reproach, and her hands raised in deprecation.

"Aren't you ashamed of yourselves?" she burst forth, in ringing tones. "You, who call yourselves honest men, and loyal citizens! You

who come here with a claim for fair play, you
who come here to assert the right of every
American to be treated with respect by every
other ; to insult and maltreat an old man with
white hair—a man whom, as a long associate
in your work, you should honor ? Do you
come to my house to call forth a man who
was even now listening to plans for the improvement of your homes and lives and pros-
pects, simply that you may turn yourselves into
a pack of dogs to bark at him ? **Go home.**
Lay aside your prejudices and your low, unworthy passions, and think whether we be
entirely in the wrong. Think whether you are
showing yourselves worthy of being trusted ?
Go home and weigh calmly your conduct
against that of these officers, and decide for
yourselves whether you deserve to be met half-
way. And I give you my word of honor as
owner of the Shawsheen Mills, that when you
decide to behave like men and not like beasts,
you shall be treated as men. You shall have
good places with good pay. You shall find
that we are willing to do as much as—yes,
more, than you are willing to do for us, and
that we will meet you half-way in the open,

fair discussion of all points connected with the labor question."

"Three cheers for the lady!" shouted a hoodlum, who cared not which side he was on, provided he could make a noise.

But the cheers were stayed, and further demonstration was choked in utterance. For Otis Greenough fell suddenly at the feet of the woman who stood there boldly championing ' him and her sense of right.

The superintendent carried him quickly within and put him on a sofa; a physician was hastily summoned, and in a few words Villard dismissed the mob, now hushed and awe-stricken.

But Otis Greenough in one moment had passed beyond the disturbances of howling malcontents, beyond the petty smallness of his old-fashioned and cramped ideas, out into that world where there is no fear of anarchy and socialism, no disgrace in being a philanthropist, no bounds to the heart of love for all mankind, and no limits to the horizon of a larger, diviner life.

VIII.

DEATH is never fully realized until he is an actual presence ; and Otis Greenough's sudden demise before their eyes and almost under, if not by, their own hands, solemnized and terrified the mob, and brought the strikers to a sense of the desperate pass to which they had come.

The members of the Labor Union laid their grievances aside for the time, and paid every mark of respect to the old agent now that he had passed beyond the recognition of it. A sudden fit of apoplexy had blotted out his choleric and intolerant behavior, and left only the remembrance that he had been their head for many years.

But when he had been laid away in the new cemetery on Shepard Hill, the smouldering embers of discord began again to break forth into hot flames of prejudice and passion.

Geoffrey Burnham and John Villard were consulting together in the mill office the day after the funeral, when the door opened and the owner of the mills walked in.

"I have come," she said, in answer to their ill-concealed surprise, "to talk over the situation of the strike. I want the mills re-opened."

"We shall be only too happy to comply with your wishes, Miss Shepard," said Burnham, placing a chair in a comfortable light for her. "Upon what terms do you propose it?"

"I want to compromise," she answered, "and give them a better chance than they have ever had. It may take us some time to decide on the exact terms. Would it be better, do you think,"—she unconsciously turned to Villard—"to take them back on the old terms, re-instate them precisely as they were, and then go on and make our changes?"

"That would hardly do," he replied. "Experience has proved them very jealous of new methods, and unwilling to consent to untried theories. If we yield everything they demand now, we shall establish a bad precedent; eh, Burnham?"

"Decidedly, and we shall meet with opposition if we undertake any changes. If there is to be a remodeling of the old system, it had better come now."

"There must be a remodeling, it seems to me," urged Salome. "Dear Mr. Greenough acted wisely, so far as he could, no doubt; but I feel that the time is come to make decided changes here. Perhaps I am not very clear in regard to them, even in my own mind. But I have some idea of what I want, and I shall be glad to have you both state your convictions and objections, if you have them, relating to everything I propose."

"It will be no light matter," said Burnham, "to select a plan and perfect it at once. It must be a work of time and much thought. Still, what is your idea?"

"I want to put the relations between us and the employes," Salome went on, "on a better footing—an ethical basis, if you like the term. We must combine the question 'Will it pay?' with a higher one, 'Is it right?'"

The two men looked at each other. Burnham bit his lip.

"I do not propose to promise the people an era of absolute prosperity and uninterrupted.

progress, and let them take it as a blind destiny without exertion or sacrifice or patriotism on their part. I want to teach them to be healthy, intelligent, and virtuous citizens, and to expect from us the treatment such citizens deserve. I believe that such a course is for the pecuniary interests of the mill, as well as for theirs. I have heard enough of the conflicting interests of labor and capital; and on the other hand I do not believe in the twaddle that proclaims them one. I believe they are reciprocal, and that we must take that idea as fundamental."

"You propose a radical change, I fear." Geoffrey Burnham's tone held a new respect for this woman whom he had believed wrapped up in the toils of worldly and shallow aims.

" Yes, I may as well own it ; I do," assented Salome. "Among my grandfather's manuscripts, I came across, the other day, these sentences : 'I would like to prove my luminous ideal of what a superintendent may be among his people. I would like to live long enough to show the world that the spirit of the Crucified may rule in a cotton-mill as fully as in the life of a saint.' That sentence, gentlemen, must speak for me. In those words lies the germ of my plan of action."

Silence followed her. Geoffrey Burnham told himself that a new era must be dawning,— the era foreshadowing the millennium, since she who held the power could so bravely avow her intentions to make the Shawsheen Mills an experiment in what he called Christian social- ism. But John Villard, after a moment, rose and extended his hand to Salome.

"I pledge my hearty co-operation," he said, "and thank God for the opportunity to prove what a cotton-mill may become by the new Christian political economy."

"Thank you," said Salome. "And now let us see just what the strikers demand, and how far we can grant their wishes."

John Villard produced the paper which had been presented on the first day of the strike, and placed it in Salome's hands. It was the first time she had seen it. She read it through very carefully.

"It seems to me there was no need of these long months of idleness," she commented, when she had finished the paper. "Now, let us see. First, they demand recognition, as the Shawsheen Labor Union. I think we may yield that point, safely enough."

" Without modification ?" inquired Geoffrey Burnham.

" Why not ? "

" They will take advantage of us. They will dictate and become arbitrary. The Labor Union grows by what it feeds on. It will become an elephant on our hands."

" Not if they have something better to take its place," said Salome. " I am fully persuaded that they will meet us half-way, if we give them a union that is better than theirs. Let their union alone for the present."

" I am with you there," said Villard. " It devolves upon us to change its character into something that shall be, at least, as helpful as they *want* to make this one."

" Next, the ten-hour system," pursued Salome, who was not yet ready to discuss the improved union. " Certainly there can be no possible objection against granting this clause?"

" Certainly not," said Burnham, feeling himself appealed to.

" ' The new frames must be taken out and

the mules replaced, with a written agreement
that no more of the obnoxious machinery shall
be added for five years.' That seems rather
arbitrary. How is it, Mr. Villard?"

"It is arbitrary," he responded. "The
frames must be retained. We must be allowed
to adopt improved machines and methods, or
where shall we be in this age of competition?
But I think there will be little trouble with
the men, if I am allowed to approach them in
the right way. Anyhow, I will try."

"Do so," was the reply. "Make them see
that improved methods are for their interest as
much as for ours. As to the wage-section—
were their wages actually cut down?"

"Yes," replied both men.

"That must not be allowed," said Salome.
"The mills were paying a handsome profit
when this was done, weren't they?"

"They were," said Villard. "Better than
for a year before."

"Give them their old pay, with the under-
standing that wages will be increased when
work is heavier. I propose to myself a wild
scheme of profit-sharing, or a sliding scale of
wages, in the future."

"Good," cried Villard. "The very thing I've been wanting to try. I believe in it heartily. But where did you get the idea of it?"

"Oh, I've been reading all the practical articles I could find on political economy, as applied to mills and factories, for some months," Salome replied, "and I have evolved some queer theories, I fear; but I propose to give them a fair trial, unless you pronounce them too visionary. I am glad you approve of profit-sharing. And you, Mr. Burnham?"

"I approve of making the experiment," said the more cautious superintendent. "I do not jump at conclusions. Nevertheless, the idea, though new, looks practicable, and I should like to see it tried."

"They have already tried it in one or two places where it is proving a great success, I believe," said Salome. "You know the experiment was tried as long ago as 1831, when Mr. John S. Vandeleur put it into effect successfully in County Clare, Ireland. The Paris and Orleans Railway Company began to share profit with its employes in 1844, and the Maison Leclaire, I think, two years before, both of which have proved very successful. I do not see why we cannot adopt it."

"We can," asserted Villard, confidently. "It is already being tried on a small scale by several firms in this country. Why should not we join the procession?"

"What are you going to do about the demand for weekly wages?" asked Burnham.

"What objections are there?" Salome asked.

"It will entail extra expense for clerks and book-keepers," responded Burnham. "That seems unnecessary."

"The men claim that they have to depend in great measure on the credit system at the stores," explained Villard. "Their wages coming only once a month, they get short of money. If sickness or other additional expense comes upon them, they are often seriously inconvenienced by lack of their rightful wages. Again, if they are able to put a little money in the savings-bank, why should they not have the benefit of the interest that accrues through the month, rather than we? The money is theirs."

"On the other hand," interrupted Burnham, "those men whose first duty, on being paid off, seems to lie in getting gloriously drunk, would have the opportunity just four times as often."

"We have a work to do in that direction," said Salome in a pained voice. "In a sense we are our brother's keepers. I half believe that the solution of the temperance question is largely in the control of the employers of labor; and that the secondary, and often the primary, causes of intemperance are bad and unwholesome food, which create a craving for drink; bad company, which tempts it; squalid houses, which drive men forth for cheerfulness; and the want of more comfortable places of resort which leaves them no refuge but the saloons. It is in our power to remedy all these evils. Give them good sanitation, well-ventilated houses, comfortable homes, and reading-rooms, and coffee-parlors, and only the most depraved will be tempted by the low saloons."

"But, Miss Shepard, surely you do not propose all these things?" and Geoffrey Burnham looked his astonishment.

"Why not?" was the terse reply.

"Where will your profits come in? You cannot afford it."

Salome smiled. Her money was her own. Why should she not use it as she pleased?

"No. For the first year or two I shall not pocket an immense profit; that is true," she assented. "But I am not likely to come to want. And Newbern Shepard's mills must be put on the basis where he desired, above all things, to see them during his life-time. He planned a noble scheme. It is my birthright and my duty to carry it into effect. It will cost me something to get the mills where they must be; but it will pay in the end. Of that I feel sure."

"You are quite right," said John Villard. "What may we not hope for when the condition of the working-people shall receive that concentrated attention which has hitherto been devoted to the more favored ranks? When charity, which has, for ages past, done so much mischief, shall learn to do good? When the countless pulpits of our country, which have always been so active in preaching Catholicism or Anglicism, Calvinism or Armenianism, and all other isms, shall preach pure and simple Christianity? When, by a healthy environment of the toiling masses, and the exercise of hygienic sense and science, mankind shall be healthy and free from questionable instincts and morbidly exaggerated appetites? I tell you, we cannot even approach an estimate of the extent to which every improvement, social, moral or material, reacts on the nation's ethical and intellectual progress, and the prosperity of her industries."

"But you are taking us entirely away from the question in hand," said Geoffrey Burnham, "which was, shall we grant the demand for weekly wages?"

"Not so far away as you seem to think," retorted Villard. "The questions of sanitation and morality affect them, and us too, as well as the question of weekly wages. As for the latter, I am in favor of trying it on."

"So am I," said Salome. "I am in favor of trying every new method until we can know positively which are the best ones."

"With modifications," said Burnham, smiling at her vehemence. "I don't exactly approve of the weekly system, but the majority are against me, and I may as well cast my vote with yours. Shall we send for their committee, then, and offer them all concessions, except those relating to the spinning-frames?"

"Yes, I should do so," said Salome, "and prepare to open the mills at once, provided they decide to accept our terms."

"That is practically decided already," laughed Burnham, "by our accepting theirs. Villard, you may negotiate with them about the frames. They are inclined to listen to you better than to me, for some reason."

"They know I've been in their place," said Villard. "That makes all the difference in the world to them. They think I understand their side of the question; that is all."

"Then you will confer with them immediately?" said Salome, rising to go. "And will you make all necessary preparations to open the mills? And then will you confer with me?"

"Most certainly, Miss Shepard." Geoffrey Burnham spoke for both of them. "But— I beg your pardon, you have not spoken of a new agent. We must have one, you know. I trust you have made some wise selection?"

"I am prepared to surprise you," Salome replied, buttoning her glove. "You two men will oblige me by transacting all necessary busi-

7

ness for the present, in your positions of first
and second superintendents, and by looking
closely after the thousand details which I do
not yet understand. Meanwhile, I shall come
to the office every day and, with your co-operation and kind help, shall learn the business.
I have too many schemes for the general
improvement of the Shawsheen Mills and its
operatives, to trust the mills in the hands of
a stranger. I propose to be my own agent.
Good-morning."

Salome Shepard never looked handsomer, or
smiled more sweetly, than she did when she
uttered the last sentence, and closed the door
behind her, leaving her two completely astonished hearers standing in the middle of the
office.

"Whe-e-w!" ejaculated Geoffrey Burnham,
after a little. "How does that strike you?
The Shawsheen Mills run by a 'female woman,'
as A. Ward would put it! And, by George!
we are expected to stay and work,—under a
woman!"

John Villard broke into a peal of laughter.
"It's awfully funny at first," he said, calm-
ing down again. "But, after all, why not?

She isn't the empty-headed, aimless creature
we thought her. She's read and studied, and
has some very sound notions."

"But, Villard—a woman-agent!" gasped
Burnham. "We shall be the laughing-stock
of the whole state."

"Let them laugh," answered Villard. "They
laugh best who laugh last. And with her
notions, her thirst for further knowledge, her
enthusiasm, and, above all, her money, the
Shawsheen Mills will be in a position at the
end of a few years to do the laughing, while
those who laugh at us now will set to studying
our methods and come to us for advice."

"But she knows nothing of the practical
part of mill-economy," objected Burnham. "The
mills will go to rack and ruin. Jove! Old
Mr. Greenough would turn over in his grave
if he could have heard her as she stopped
in the door and said: 'I propose to be my
own agent.' A woman!"

"I know," replied Villard, "that it will
seem odd, and perhaps uncomfortably so, at first,
to acknowledge her as head. But, after all,
she does not propose to dictate as to the
business itself."

" She will," interrupted Burnham. " Women always do. She will jump at conclusions, mistake her inferences for logical deductions and the wisdom which comes only with experience, and, after the first month, will know more than we do. I know women. They are impulsive and illogical ; and they can't subvert nature and become good business men."

"No ; but they may prove good business women," was Villard's answer. " We do not know, yet, what she can or what she will do. I believe she will be willing to leave the details of the business to us yet, for a long time. She is not a conceited woman ; and although she has the faculty common to her sex of making some surprising jumps at conclusions, I do not believe her to be obstinate about them. She proposes to make a study of the business, and realizes that this is a work of years. And, besides, what will save the mills is this : she has an extended plan in manuscript of her grandfather's scheme for making this an ideal institution. If she is willing to leave the business to us for the present, and is capable of adapting Newbern Shepard's theories of years ago to the needs of to-day, we are all

right, Jeff; and a new era is about to begin
for the Shawsheen Mills."

"I only hope we may like it," assented
Burnham doubtfully. "And now for the
conference with the Labor Union."

IX.

MARION SHAW was one of those women whose
lives are a constant giving of their best, with
no thought of return.   We have all seen such
women.   From the self-sacrificing maiden aunt
in the humblest home, up to the Florence
Nightingales and Dorothea Dixes of the world,
they are God's angels, everywhere, to suffering
humanity.

Marion Shaw and Salome Shepard had been
in boarding-school together ; and although the
former had been left from the start to support
herself and her widowed mother, the friendship
between the two girls had never abated.

Marion's mother had died a year before, and
something material had dropped out of life
for the girl.   Grief and the solitude which
ensued after her mother's death told upon her
constitution ; and when Salome's letter of invi-

tation reached her, it was like a boon from Heaven. She threw up her situation in Madame Blanc's private school and went to Shepardtown, arriving there late in the evening, before Salome's visit to the counting-room.

When the latter came home they settled cosily in Salome's room for an " old-time talk," such as they had enjoyed as girls.

" Why didn't you let me know you were tired to death with that interminable teaching ?" asked Salome. "I should have had you come to me long ago. You are as pale as a ghost."

" Oh, I'm all right now," answered Marion, who never cared to talk of herself. " Tell me about the strike here. I read of it in a Boston newspaper, when it came on, and again when Mr. Greenough died. But, after the fashion of newspapers with regard to anything you care particularly to follow up, they dropped the subject the minute one's interest was roused. And your letter was so meager ! Yes, it was. You only write the barest details, and not too many of them. Is the strike ended ? "

" No, but I hope it will be before night," Salome replied. " I've given orders this morning that a compromise be made at once. Yes, don't stare at me, please. Why shouldn't I give orders? They're my mills."

"I'm not staring. It's vulgar to stare, and the lady professors at Mme. Blanc's fashionable boarding-school do not stare. Why, it would be as much as their position is worth!" retorted Marion. "Yes, they're your mills, I suppose, and a handsome piece of property they are too, in the eyes of poor me, who own only the clothes on my back. But, pardon me, dear, it does seem a little odd to hear Salome Shepard, the most exclusive and the most fashionable girl at school, talk about giving orders in a cotton-mill. You're not getting strong-minded, are you, dear?"

"If to begin to take an active interest in two thousand souls, who are dependent upon my money and the business interests it represents, is to become strong-minded, I'm afraid I shall have to plead guilty." Salome looked narrowly at her friend. Possibly she had mistaken her, and their sympathies were farther apart than she had hoped.

"Bless you!" responded Marion heartily, "I'm strong-minded myself; want to vote and all that. Don't believe intemperance and lots of other evils will ever be subdued in this country, until women have something to say, and say it through the ballot-box. It is not so very dreadful when you once get on to that platform, is it?"

"Oh, I hadn't thought of voting particularly," Salome hastened to answer. "I don't really think I want that. But I do want to do something for my people."

"And you'll find," retorted Marion, "before you've gone very far, that if you had the power of legislation, you could help them ten times as well."

"Possibly," Salome answered, doubtfully. "But, Marion, there are so many things absolutely necessary to be done for the Shawsheen operatives. If you could see them and the homes they live in, the temptations to which they are exposed, the poverty in which they live!"

"And you propose to go to work among them,—to reform them?"

"Yes, God helping me; them and the factory system together. Behold me," said Salome, rising to her full height, and putting on a mock-tragic air: "Behold and see: Salome Shepard, Reformer.   That's my platform."

"Salome, dear, what do you mean?"   Mrs. Soule had just come in.   "Don't mind her, Marion, she delights in hearing herself talk like a suffrage leader, lately.   I don't approve of it, as she knows; but I can only wait for the mood to pass."

"Which it never will, aunty dear," Salome hastened to say.   "So long as I live and am in a condition to work for the people who need substantial and material aid, as these people do, my life will be devoted to their service.   I cannot go on living the aimless, indifferent life which has been mine ever since I left school. I must have some active interest, or I shall stagnate, or, worse still, settle into a cold, hard, selfish woman of the world.   Unfortunately I was born with a heart; unfortunately for your ideal of the proper young lady of the period, I was born with a conscience, and this conscience tells me that my fortune was given me only in trust.   It is not mine for selfish enjoyment alone; it is mine to make the world better and happier and purer."

"And you are going to work among those

miserable drunken operatives," said her aunt
coldly, "whose sordid lives, and ungrateful
hearts, the whole of them, are not worth the
effort of even one month of your life, even if
you were at all a capable woman of affairs, a
woman of judgment and discretion, a woman
of sound business sense,—which you are not."

"Yes, 'among the drunken miserable operatives,'" replied Salome, ignoring the latter part
of her aunt's speech. "Among those sordid
lives and ungrateful hearts, that were worth
the Christ's dying, and for whom He worked,
living."

"You don't think of joining the Salvation
Army, I hope?" exclaimed her aunt, quite
beside herself at this new development of her
niece's purposes.

Salome laughed.

"I shall hardly have the time, aunty. I've
accepted a position at the Shawsheen Mills."

"A position?" gasped Mrs. Soule. "Oh,
Salome! Who offered you—who *dared* offer
you a *position?*"   .

"The fair owner of the mills offered it,"
answered Salome, enjoying the situation to
its fullest extent. "And I accepted, aunty.

Marion, in me you see the agent of the Shawsheen Mills ! "

Marion Shaw rose and clasped her friend
closely to her bosom. She admired her splendid courage and avowed principles, and hon-
ored this woman, with money and leisure at her
command, who was willing and anxious to de-
vote her life to service for others. But not so
Mrs. Soule.

She applied a delicate mull and lace hand-
kerchief to her eyes, and wept to think to what
an end had come her years of training; her
careful watch, that Salome should never, by any
chance, come in contact with a lower world;
her lifelong aim to make of Salome the perfect
being prescribed by her somewhat limited and
narrowed rules of ladyhood.

She begged; she pleaded; she argued; she
threatened ; she resorted to ridicule ; but
Salome stood firm, and now laughingly and
then earnestly defended the course she had
taken.

" It's of no use, aunty, as you see, for us to
argue the case. I do not forget all your kindness and love for me ; but I must choose for
myself," she said, finally. " I am old enough

to decide questions of right and wrong. Hereafter we will not argue any more. I must do this; you must submit; and that is all there is about it. Now, let's make up and be friends," and she bent down and kissed her aunt on both cheeks, as she used to do when she was a little girl.

"You, a child of Cora de Bourdillon's!" murmured her aunt, softening a little.

"Cora de Bourdillon was my mother," said Salome. "But before and above all else, Newbern Shepard was my grandfather. I am like him. I must be like him. And you must submit to the laws of heredity."

So there was never any more prolonged discussion between them. Salome's nature being so much the stronger, kind-hearted, weak Mrs. Soule could not oppose her further. But many times, in after years, was she heard to deplore the fact that Cora de Bourdillon's child was so thorough-going an epitome of Newbern Shepard.

"A good man," she would say. "A perfectly honest and well-meaning man; but not like Us!"

.

X.

EARLY that evening Geoffrey Burnham and
John Villard were announced.   Mrs. Soule and
Salome were alone in the parlors when they
came in, but Marion was sent for.

"And you've brought good news ?" asked
Salome.   "They've consented to go to work
again ? "

"Of course," Burnham replied.   "They
were only too glad to meet us on any sort of
terms."

"Wait till my friend comes down," said
Salome.   "She is interested, and will want to
hear the details.   Oh, here she is.   Miss Shaw,
allow me to present my two confrères (and
teachers as well), Mr. Burnham and Mr. Villard."

"And so it is really settled ?" Salome asked,
"and the mills are to be opened again ?"

"Monday morning, if you like," replied Burnham, " or earlier.   But to-day is Wednesday, and there are many things to be done where the mills have stood idle for months."

" I'm so glad," returned Salome.

" There is hearty rejoicing throughout the corporation," said Villard. "I was coming through there to-night and met a couple of little boys with bundles of groceries in their arms. The smallest looked up and smiled. 'We're going to have a good supper of meat and potato to-night,' he said. 'The mills are going to open and pa's got work.' I asked him how long since he had had meat, and he said not since Christmas ; and even then he only had a turkey's wing that somebody gave him."

" Poor boy ! Tell me about your conference with the Labor Union."

" It passed off smoothly," Villard went on. "Burnham told him we came from you, and were prepared to make terms with them.   We only saw the committee you know, and they are to lay our terms before the Union to-night ; but there is no doubt that they will accept. They are really very sensible and shrewd, those fellows on the committee, eh, Burnham?"

" Remarkably," replied the first superintendent. " I didn't know we had such intelligent
men."

" But it is our business to know it," Villard
returned, and Salome nodded her head. " We
laid our plans before them, and told them
that we would concede all their wishes, except
about the machinery of course. And one of
their own number spoke up promptly and said
it was hot-headed bigotry on their part that
had made them stick for the removal of the
frames. And that most of them, even the
Lancaster spinners, had come to see that every
improvement to the mills meant an improvement of their condition. Then the secretary
wanted to know if they were to be allowed to
exist as a Union. Burnham told them that you
were taking a great interest in the management
of the mills ; and that we all believe that no
harm can come of their organizing themselves into an association, provided they were
willing to be reasonable, and to confer with us
before taking extreme measures again. He
begged them to believe that you are their
friend, and want them all to have a fair chance.
And he ended by assuring them that we, as

superintendents, fully concurred with you ; and
that he hoped they would be willing to start on
a new basis, and to consider our interests as
they expect and desire us to remember theirs.
Burnham did himself proud, Miss Shepard, and
I could see they were a good deal affected by
his conduct."

"I am covered with blushes," declared
Burnham. "Spare my modesty."

"Blushing must be a novel sensation to
you," retorted Villard. "The leaders shook
hands with us when we came away and
thanked us for what we had said, assuring
us that they would be ready to enter the
mills again at once. And a different spirit
is evident to-night, all through the corporation."

"Don't be too sanguine," interrupted Burnham. "We're not through the woods yet.
And there are several ends to be achieved
before the millennium dawns."

"I should like," said Salome, "if it will
not bore you too much, to outline the general
plan I have formed for raising the condition of
things at the mills."

"Nothing would give us greater pleasure

8

than such a proof of your confidence," replied
Burnham.

"And we can assure you beforehand," said
Villard, "of our hearty co-operation."

No one but Salome noticed that her aunt
had quietly slipped away when she spoke of
her plan. Mrs. Soule did not care to hear
Salome "talk shop."

"In the first place," Salome began, "are
the mills all they should be? Are they well
lighted, aired and drained? Is the machinery
such as to benefit both the operators and the
business interests of the mills?"

"No, they are not quite up to modern
standards," Villard replied, promptly.

"I don't know," pursued Burnham, "but
they are quite as good as the average. There
are many worse mills than the Shawsheen."

"That isn't the point," Salome replied.
"Are there any better? Or are they capable
of improvement?"

"Well, yes, if you don't consider expense,"
assented Burnham.

"Are they well-lighted? Are their sanitary
conditions good?"

"They are very well-lighted indeed," said

Villard; "your grandfather built much in advance of his time, and the mills are all light and strong. But they need better ventilation in cold weather; and, as you know, sanitary science in Newbern Shepard's day was hardly up to modern demands."

"I propose putting in the best drainage system we can find. I propose bath-rooms, wash-rooms and elevators."

"Good!" said both her superintendents.

"As for machinery, you will know what is needed there. We want the latest improved methods of doing our work. It will not do for us to be behind the times, or the world will laugh at our philanthropic efforts. The standard of the mills must be as high now as it was in my grandfather's day. Nothing but the best of goods, made after the most approved modern methods, must go out from us. Otherwise the world will say we are visionary and lack good business sense."

"That is true," assented Burnham. "The business must not suffer."

"At the same time, I want the mills made so pleasant and comfortable that our operatives will prefer them to any other, knowing that we propose to consult their interests and happiness in little things, as we desire that they shall consult ours in great. Then their homes. Those old rickety tenement houses must be abolished from the face of the earth."

"Hear, hear," cried Villard, "they have long been an eyesore to me."

"They are a disgrace to us," was Salome's emphatic answer.

"But you can't do that all at once," said Burnham. "That is something that will take time."

"It is April now," said Salome. "I propose to begin at once on new houses for the operatives. They will have to stay where they are for the summer, but by cold weather I mean that every one of them shall be in new quarters."

"Whew!" said Burnham; "you *are* a woman of business, Miss Shepard. But you will have your hands full this year to build new houses for two thousand people."

"It can be done though," Villard replied. "There are plenty of carpenters and builders to be had. What kind of tenements do you propose?"

"I have not fully decided. At first I thought of having single cottages for every family, with a tiny plot of land for each. But sometimes I wonder if some of the plans for model tenement houses would not be more feasible. What do you think?"

"There are advantages in both," said Burnham. "It is doubtful if many of the operatives would appreciate a whole house, or take good care of one. On the other hand, the best tenement house system in the world has its drawbacks."

"In a country-place where there is room enough, as there is here," advised Villard, "it seems to me that the single cottage system is the better. Each family can then have a certain privacy, impossible to the tenement house system. They can soon be educated up to caring for their places, and, I think, will soon come to take pride in them. They may not pay, at first; but they will serve a higher purpose. I have thought it would be a fine thing,—in the Utopia of which I have often dreamed,—if, connected with such a factory as this, could be built some substantial, inexpensive cottages which could be sold to the work-

ing-men with families, on very easy terms.
Let them occupy them as tenants, for instance,
until their rentals amount to a certain sum—
say two hundred dollars,—unless they have
been fortunate enough to have saved that
amount, which they can pay down, and then
let them take a deed of the place and give us
a mortgage. Pardon me, Miss Shepard, I am
only supposing a case."

"And quite a supposable one," said Salome,
her eyes glowing. "Why can't it be done?"

"Doubtful if any of them would burden
themselves with a debt like that," demurred
Burnham.

"I think they would," Villard responded.
"The desire for a home of one's own is an instinct which is implanted in every human breast.
If the steadier, more sensible men of the mills
could be induced to try it, it would soon become the ambition of all the younger ones to
own their homes. I am sure the overseers, at
least, would like to try it. So many of our
operatives live in a hand-to-mouth fashion,
never saving anything. Let them see that
what they pay for rent will be credited
to them; that they are actually saving that

money, and they will, for the most part, gladly fall in with the scheme. And when a man begins to save up money, and to feel that he is worth something, his self-respect increases and ambition makes a man of him. I tell you, I believe the thing could be done here, and the condition of our working-men be vastly improved by it."

"We will, at least, make the experiment," said Salome earnestly. "At first a wild dream came to me of building model tenement houses and practically giving them the rent. But I soon came to see that it would be better for them to pay what they could afford for improved conditions."

"That would be far wiser," said Villard. "To make them objects of charity would be to lower their condition in the long run."

"Then I have a plan for the girls," Salome went on. "So many of them live in those dreadful boarding-houses. I've been into one, and I wonder how any girl can keep her self-respect and live there. I am going to build a large building, which shall have plenty of light, airy bed-rooms, prettily and inexpensively furnished; so that a girl may feel that she has a

cosy little spot somewhere on earth of her very
own. I am going to have model bath-rooms
and a large, cheerful dining-room. There will
be a matron to the establishment who will be
like a mother to the girls; not one who will
care nothing whether her girls are sober and
respectable, or miserable and besotted, so
long as they pay. This woman will win the
confidence of the girls, and lead them into
habits of personal cleanliness and common
sense; she will take an interest in their little
personal affairs, and advise them kindly and
judiciously. In short, she will make a home
for them in the truest sense of the word."

"You will have to have her made to order,
Salome," interrupted Marion from the sofa where
she had been an interested listener. "Such
paragons do not exist."

"And would scarcely be appreciated by the
average factory girl if they did," added Burnham, smiling at Marion.

"I shall have a large and pleasant parlor
with a piano and a comfortable reading-room,"
Salome continued, as though not hearing; "I
don't suppose the girls, judging from what I
hear and see of them, will care much for read-

ing at first; but if I put plenty of light, healthful literature in their way, with illustrated books
and good pictures on the walls, they will
gradually come to like them.   And then, there
must be weekly entertainments, and perhaps a
hall."

"And what about the young men?" inquired
Villard.   "Are you going to leave our sex out
in the cold?"

"Yes, if you educate the girls so much above
them, what are the young fellows to do?"

"They shall have such a boarding-house
too," said Salome, "only we'll call them
Unions.   I hate the name boarding-house,
and I should think they would; and then, by
and by, there are still other schemes in my mind.
There are children, plenty of them, on the
corporation.   They are poor, sickly, unkempt,
uncared-for.   All this must be changed."

"That will come, I think," said Burnham,
"with their improved conditions and surroundings.   It is unhealthful where they now are.
Shall you build the new houses there?"

"Oh, no, I forgot to say," answered Salome,
"that we must put up their new quarters on
the hill, the other side of the mills.   It is much

pleasanter up there, and a far more healthful
locality.   Work on them can begin right away.
Will you find me the proper man to undertake
the building of the houses, Mr. Villard ? "

John Villard's heart fairly burned with enthusiasm.   This was a project he had long
cherished, although he had been entirely
without means or prospect of ever being able
to carry it out.

" You may be sure I will do my best," he
answered.

" And we will reserve the power of directing
and planning the buildings ourselves," she added.

" I'm glad you're going to do something for
the children," said Marion.   " If you don't
succeed in improving things in this generation
much, you will in the next, if you educate the
children."

" That is what I propose to do," said Salome.
" They must have better schools than they ever
had."

" And be compelled to attend them," inter-
posed Burnham.

" Oh, there are so many things to be done.   It
will take years to get everything in working
order."

"You have laid out a beautiful scheme, Miss Shepard," remarked Geoffrey Burnham, "and in most respects a practical one. But you must not be too sanguine. These people are ignorant,—fairly steeped in ignorance. They are jealous, too, and doubtless will mistrust your motives, and believe you have some selfish reason behind all your endeavor."

"I have," laughed Salome. "I want my mills to be models, and my people to be the best, most skilled, most intelligent, and most progressive community in America."

"Bravo!" said Villard. "So do I."

"I am not so sanguine as you may think," Salome went on. "I know they are ignorant. How should they be anything else? All their lives they've been used as we use the machines in the factory,—to make good cloth, and plenty of money. Nobody has thought of their welfare, or cared what they did, or thought, or became, when working-hours were over. How do we know what sort of men they are, or what capabilities they possess? I read somewhere, only the other day, that there may still be Fichtes tending geese, and Robert Burns' toiling on the farm; that there may be, yet, successors

of William Dean Howells at the type-forms, of
T. B. Aldrich at the book-keeper's desk, of
Mark Twain at the pilot-wheel. We have no
right to keep them back. But this writer went
on to say, that the world has less need of them,
even, than of those who cannot aspire to thrive
outside the shop, and who go to their daily toil
knowing that their highest hope must be not
to get 'out of a job' and not to have their
wages cut. I don't suppose they will, at once,
appreciate our efforts to better their condition.
Possibly they will oppose us at first; but we
can have no better task to perform than to
make them prosperous, contented and joyous
in their work. And by making a man of the
operative, I fully believe we shall bring material
prosperity to the mills."

"But the expense," urged Burnham. "Have
you calculated that? I doubt if the mills could
stand so heavy a burden all at once."

"I have calculated the expense," Salome
answered him. "And what cannot be done from
the yearly profits of the mills, I will do myself."

"We shall be eagerly watched by the whole
manufacturing world," said Burnham.

"So much the better," added Villard. "It

is time somebody set the example. If we succeed in carrying out all these plans, and keep the mills on a paying basis as well, it will be the beginning of a mighty reform in the working-man's world. I believe we can succeed."

"You will be called quixotic and all sorts of pleasant things, Salome," said her friend Marion.

"The beginner in any reform is always called a crank, if nothing worse," replied Salome. "If I chose to build a million dollar castle to live in myself; if I preferred to dress in cloth of gold and silver; if I insisted upon eating off solid gold dishes; or even if I were to endow a church or a female college, the world would admire and praise me, and say these things are a rich woman's prerogative. If I choose instead to spend my fortune on the Shawsheen Mills, and elevate by its judicious expenditure two thousand operatives for whom I ought to feel morally and socially responsible, the world will probably wonder and call me quixotic. Christ Himself was called a fanatic. Most people to-day, if they voiced their real sentiments, would wonder that He could be so democratic as to die for the whole world, ignorant, uncultivated, detestable sinners, and all."

One of those silences fell upon the room, that always follows the mention of Christ's name in a conversation not strictly " religious " in character. Marion was admiring the courage of her friend; Burnham was rather taken aback at this fearless reference to a Being whom he seldom heard mentioned outside the churches; and Villard was surprised and delighted with this unworldly woman of the world, and her avowal of principles and hopes and wishes which he had cherished for years. He was the first to speak.

" You must have done some hard thinking, —and a good deal of reading, in the past six months."

" Yes," answered Salome. " I have. I have read everything I could think or hear of, on subjects bearing on this case; and I have lain awake many a night, since it was really borne in upon me that I have something to do here, planning my work. But the greater part of the credit, if there is any, in my plans, lies with my grandfather. He thought out many of these things, years ago; I have simply adapted his theories to our modern times and conditions."

XI.

AND so the great strike ended.

Had Salome realized the burden of care which she was taking upon herself, it is doubtful whether she would have assumed it as cheerfully as she did. But as weeks rolled into months, and responsibilities multiplied and cares increased until she became as hard a worker as any in the mills, she did not flinch. She had put her hand to the plough, and it did not once occur to her to turn back.

She went to the office of the mills the day they were opened, and began to study, thoroughly, the details of the business. Villard and Burnham were her teachers, and both were often astonished at her business keenness and cool judgment. She had pressed Marion into service immediately, and always took her to the counting-room, where the two staid throughout the entire morning, going home to lunch at two, and usually remaining there the rest of the day. But always, whether she was in the house, or out driving, or overseeing the new houses, which were progressing rapidly, Salome's one thought was the improvement of conditions at the Shawsheen Mills.

When Marion had been with her a week, Salome said to her :

" Marion, I want you to stay with me all the time."

" I should be so glad," replied her friend, " but I can't afford it. I shall have to go out into the world again, before long, to earn my living, dear; but I will stay here as long as I can."

" You good girl!" was Salome's answer. " Why not stay here and earn your living? I want a companion, shall very soon need a secretary, and as soon as I get things in running order, ought to have a woman like you to help draw in my people. You need a congenial place at a comfortable salary. Now, why not stay? I will pay you a thousand dollars a year."

Marion drew a breath of astonishment.

"It isn't worth that," she said; "Madame Blanc only paid me seven hundred."

"Madame Blanc is not fixing a scale of wages for me," said Salome; "as to your 'worth,' my dear, I must judge of that. When we get fairly at work, I shall give you enough to do, and you will find yourself a very busy woman. Besides, if I had a young man to do what I want you to do for me, he would ask a thousand dollars, wouldn't he? And why shouldn't you have it? Because you are a woman?"

Marion was not demonstrative. On the contrary, she had a great deal of the true New England reserve; but she got up and went over to her friend, put both arms around her neck and then——cried.

"If you could know what a chance this is for me!" she said at last. "If you had known what a dreary thing existence had become, and what a hopeless prospect I had in the future! And now, to live here and work with you,—in your grand scheme,—Oh, Salome!" And she wept again.

"Then I will put the care of the cottages into your hands first of all," said Salome, patting

9

her cheek. " You've kept house and know what one ought to be like for an ordinary family,—what things are necessary for the comfort of the household and convenience of the housewife. I don't. I should be as apt to build expensive music-rooms and leave out the pantries, as any way. Go ahead, and get up as nice houses as you can, at $1,500, $2,000 and $2,500 a piece. Mr. Villard thinks none of the employes will care to buy anything more expensive. Here is the architect's address," and she handed Marion a card.

But the building of the model boarding-house was a project too dear to Salome's heart for her to easily relinquish to others. Her plan, as she had presented it to Villard and Burnham, grew and magnified itself until her co-laborers had to resort to all sorts of arguments to keep her from wild extravagance.

She had begun by planning for the factory-girls a house which should be really a home; but as she went about among the operatives, and began to get an inkling of what the young men of the mills really were, of the bare, desolate dens which gave them shelter, she did not wonder that they resorted to the streets for comfort and amusement. She began to see how the young men and girls who entered the mills could scarcely help drifting into low and unworthy lives; and she grew more determined to do something to raise them to a higher plane of living.

Her grandfather's manuscripts did not help her much here. In Newbern Shepard's day, the factory-hand had not sunk to such ignorance or even degradation, as he has, in some instances, in later times; and in those more democratic times, it had not been so hard for him to rise above the level of his kind. In that day, too, it had been possible for him to find a home, in the true sense of the word, with families of a certain degree of refinement. But in Salome's more modern times, she saw, and grieved, that the factory boarding-places were of the sort that dragged the operatives down and kept them on a lower plane, even, than the Shawsheen tenement system.

She consulted much with the superintendents and with Marion. She visited the large cities and thoroughly examined the young men's and young women's various houses and unions. She got ideas from all, but a perfected plan from none. Finally, she collaborated with her architect, Robert Fales, and soon had her model boarding-house on paper. After that it was only a work of days to begin on the foundations of the institution.

The operatives at the Shawsheen Mills gazed on all these changes with curious interest, which, however, they carefully suppressed when any of their superiors were about. The average independent American citizen, as he exists among workingmen, does not care to pose as an object of even partial charity. He delights in crying out against Capital, and clamoring for a share of the Profits; but when it comes to actual taking of what he does not feel he has earned, he is more backward.

The Shawsheen operatives, in spite of the promises which had been made, had gone to work again with little hope that the state of affairs for them would be any better in future than in the past. As days went by, and they saw Salome Shepard come to the mills every morning, and knew that she was personally interested in them as her people, they were skeptical of any results for good. And when they began to hear it whispered that she, a woman, was

the actual head of the Shawsheen Mills, some
of them talked earnestly of leaving. What!
they—strong, able-bodied, skilled mechanics—
work under a woman?

But they didn't go. A dull season was upon
them, and work scarce. Other mills were shut-
ting down and sending their operatives into
two months of enforced idleness. The Shawsheen hands were forced to stay where they
were and be thankful for a chance to work.

Then, as the story that they were to be
furnished with new and better homes gained
credence among them, their first real interest
dawned. Many did not believe their conditions would be bettered; many, even, did not
care; and most of them grumbled because
their rents would probably be high, and said
the new buildings were only a means to grind
the poor and extort more money from them, to
put into a rich woman's pocket. Such is the
thankless task of the philanthropist.

Salome heard something of this, but did not
allow the knowledge to disquiet her.

"A few months will convince them," she
said, quietly. "No wonder they are on the
lookout for oppression and extortion. As near

as I can judge, this factory has long been run
on a plan to warrant them in such a belief."
And this was all she ever said against Otis
Greenough's method of administering affairs
at the mills.

As the summer went by, Salome's friends in
the town began to wonder at her extravagant
outlay, as they called it. They prophesied that
she would soon tire of her new amusement, and
leave the houses unfinished, when her projects
would fall flat. Some of them came to her and
remonstrated, on the ground that her inexpe-
rience in financial affairs was cause enough for
her leaving the Shawsheen Mills and the
employes as they had been. But invariably
she replied, that if she had chosen to build
herself a million-dollar castle, they would have
approved of her; but because she proposed
to spend a half-million on the mill property,
all of which she felt sure would return to her
some day with interest, she was called extravagant and foolish.

"But if you had built the million-dollar
house," said Mrs. Greenough, "it would have
been a great thing for the place. Think what
an ornament to Shepardtown it would be!"

"And think what an improvement—what a great thing for Shepardtown—it will be to tear away those miserable, tumbledown tenements on Shawsheen alley, and to add a hundred neat and cosy houses to the hill," she retorted. "And, besides, you haven't seen my —well, my Institution (I haven't named it yet). Think what an ornament that will be to the place."

But as nobody realized what the "Institution" of her dreams was to be, Salome got no sympathy from her friends. Curiosity increased on all hands, as the summer waned and an immense brick structure grew apace on the hill. It had a square, dome-like center, with huge wings on each side. But the workmen were sworn to secrecy, and nobody was allowed to go inside from the time the building was far enough advanced to allow of its entrances being fastened up.

XII.

IT was finished at last. The plasterers and painters and plumbers had done their last stroke of work and departed, leaving the keys with Salome, as she had requested. On the same afternoon, she sent for Robert Fales, and together they showed Burnham and Villard, with Marion Shaw and Mrs. Soule—who was as anxious as any of them to see the place, although she would not own it—over the new building.

A broad flight of stone steps led up to the main entrance. The wooden framework, which had concealed the façade, had been taken down, and there, over the massive doorway, was the name of Salome's "Institution," carved in red sandstone—"NEWBERN SHEPARD HALL."

"Why not simply Shepard Hall?" said Burnham, as they stood looking up at it.

" Or Salome Shepard Hall ? " put in Mrs.
Soule's voice, for she felt that it would be like
the rest of her niece's folly to have her name
carved in stone up there.

" Auntie ! " exclaimed Salome reprovingly;
then, turning to Geoffrey Burnham—" Shepard
Hall might have meant me, or it might have
meant my father, or the whole race of us in
general. This building is a memorial to Newbern Shepard, not to his family. How do you
like the design of the façade ? "

The building was of red brick, with massive
trimmings of red sandstone, and was substantial and useful in general appearance, rather
than ornate.

" Ten times as expensive as you needed,"
was her aunt's comment.

" Yes," answered Burnham, to whom the remark was directed. " A cheap, wooden building
would have answered the purpose, I should say."

" Perhaps," laughed Salome ; " but I am not
putting up wooden monuments to my grandfather's memory. Besides, you don't know my
purpose, yet."

" Something quixotic and unnecessary, I'm
afraid, my dear," answered Mrs. Soule.

Salome did not answer but led the way up the stairway, and unlocked the heavy doors These opened into a vestibule leading into a large room fitted up with bookcases and tables.

" This is the library," said she. " Now, see the two reading-rooms, one on each side. One is for the girls, and one for the young men."

They passed out into the one designed for the girls,—a pleasant airy room with plenty of light and space. The walls were tinted and the woodwork was in the natural finish. Nothing in the way of furnishing had, of course, been done. Beyond the reading-room was another large class-room, and opening from it were several smaller ones. These all occupied one wing of the new building.

" What do you propose to have done with all these rooms ? " asked some one.

Salome looked over to John Villard and smiled.

" I've read and studied ' All Sorts and Conditions of Men ' to some purpose," she said ; " I propose, as time goes on, to have various practical and useful things taught the girls here. Dressmaking for instance, and millinery and domestic science. The conveniences for that, though, are in the basement."

She led the way by a flight of stairs that led from a side-entrance, at the end of the wing, to the basement. There was a spacious hall with rows of hooks to hang garments on. From this, opened a large and pleasant dining-room. Under the main portion of the building was a great kitchen with ranges and all the modern appliances of a hotel kitchen, though on a smaller scale.

"Isn't this rather elaborate for a factory boarding-house ? " asked Burnham; " for, I take it, that is one of your objects, at least, if not the primary one."

" I approve of this," said Mrs. Soule judicially. " It's poor policy to fit out a kitchen with cheap stuff. Give servants the best of everything to do with, and teach them how to take care of them."

" Miss Shepard has gone over the subject very carefully," said Mr. Fales, " and, I must say, has shown most excellent judgment in everything. As you say, madam, it's only money wasted to put cheap stuff into a building like this."

"Now, look through the pantries and larder and laundry," Salome interrupted; "I think, for a woman who knows absolutely nothing of the details of housekeeping, I've excelled myself." She spoke boastfully and shook her head at Marion, at the close of her speech.

"How much of it did Miss Shaw plan?" slyly asked Geoffrey Burnham.

"Every bit of it, below the main floor," responded Salome. "Since you seem incapable of believing that I did it, I may as well own that Marion and Mr. Fales planned the whole of the basement, and that I, in my ignorance, could only look on and admire. But they did so well that now I am inclined to take all the glory to myself."

They passed through the basement, coming up at the other end of the building, and found themselves in the young men's wing. Here, besides the reading-rooms and class-room, was another fitted with two or three work-benches.

"I propose to give them a chance to take an industrial education," said Salome, "if they should want it."

"I declare!" ejaculated Mrs. Soule. "To

give skilled mechanics a chance to take lessons at the work-bench ! You are out of your mind, child."

"I didn't plan it for skilled mechanics, auntie," said Salome gently, "although they may come if they want to. But you know, or ought to, that the majority of our men can only perform one kind of work. They may be nearly perfect in their special branch, but are almost helpless when it comes to handling the hammer and saw and chisel. If they learn the proper use of these things, it will not only increase their knowledge in that direction, it will broaden them in other ways."

"I don't see how," persisted her aunt.

"Besides," put in John Villard, "if it does no other good, if the experiment keeps a few of our fellows off the street at night and develops a new taste, it will be worth while."

"Well, perhaps you are right," said Mrs. Soule, "but no such philosophy or philanthropy was taught in my day."

"'The world do move,' auntie," laughed Salome. "Now, shall we go upstairs?"

A broad flight of steps from the hallway at the end of the wing led up to the second floor, which was just like the one on the girls' wing. Upstairs, the broad corridor ran through the middle of the wing, with bedrooms opening from either side. In the main body of the building, under the dome, was a large hall, fitted up with movable seats, and having a raised platform at the front.

"This is the pride of my heart," Salome announced, as she ushered her friends into it. "If any one dares to criticise it, woe be unto him! Mr. Burnham, what fault can you find with this?"

They all laughed at her inconsistency.

"I should not dare make it known, if I had any," he said. "But may I ask what it is for?"

"Why, to hold meetings in, and lectures and things," she answered, quickly; "what did you suppose?"

"Oh! And for the Labor Unions to congregate in and plan how they may overthrow and destroy you, I suppose," scoffed Burnham. "And it is a capital place to breed the next strike."

"There will be no 'next strike,'" was the confident answer. "And as for the rest, wait and see. I had the seats all movable because once in a while there will be a party, and they will want the floor for dancing."

"Salome! Not dancing?" cried her aunt.

"Why not? The floor is an excellent one for dancing. I saw to that myself," said she, purposely misunderstanding her relative.

"You are not going to let them have their low dances here?" Mrs. Soule's tone showed how much the idea horrified her.

"Low dances? Certainly not," said her niece. "But we are going to show them how to have something better. We are going to lift them above wanting a low entertainment of any kind, and teach them how such things are carried on by better people,—by us, for example."

"Salome, you don't mean me to understand that you are going to come and dance here, yourself?"

"Perhaps, though I had not thought of it. But why not?" continued the perverse niece. "Mr. Villard, will you lead the first figure with me, on our opening night?"

"With the greatest pleasure in the world,"

said he, with a thrill at his heart which he did not recognize.

Mrs. Soule sat down on a convenient window-seat.

"What would your father say?" she murmured.

"I never knew my father well enough to judge." Salome answered, with a slight tinge of bitterness in her tone. "But I know what my grandfather would say. I am going to put a piano in here,—or would you have an organ? —and I intend that this hall shall be the rallying place of the young people. I'm also going to give a course of entertainments here during the winter, twice a week; I'm not going to begin with lectures and heavy 'intellectual treats;' but I will gradually lead up to them with concerts and even a minstrel show or two."

"Salome," gasped her aunt feebly from the window-sill.

"You see, if we begin by shooting over their heads, they won't come at all," said Salome. "But if we begin with something light and amusing, and not too far above their level, and gradually raise the tone of the entertainments, they'll find themselves attending lectures and

other sugar-coated forms of intellectual better-
ment, and like them; and never mistrust that I
am working out a mission on their unsuspect-
ing heads."

"I'm glad you realize something of their
present intellectual condition," said John Villard, who had been unusually silent and grave
while looking over the new building; "and
realize that it's only gradually that we can
bring them, as a class, up to a higher grade as
intelligent young people."

" Oh, I do," said Salome, " I've seen too much
of them, myself, this summer. At first, I was
appalled by the absolute lack of common knowledge among the average girls. But there are
a few, I know, who have already improved the
slight advantages they've had ; and these few
I shall rely on to help me by their influence in
raising the rest ; the 'little leaven,' you know.
It seems to me, that only by raising the intellectual condition, and the educational aspira-
tion, can we hope to accomplish anything of
permanent value to the mills."

"That is the only way," was Villard's
response. "And, Miss Shepard," he said,
hurriedly, for the others had already scattered

through the girls' wing, leaving them alone, "I want to say that, as I believe you have found the only true solution to the main questions of the labor problem, I pledge myself to heartily sustain you in every way. You have only to command me, and I am ready."

Why did Salome turn away to hide the vivid blush that suddenly swept over her face ?

"I am sure of that," she said, presently, with an effort, "I have counted on you from the first. I shall try, by my own personal efforts, to help the factory girls. But I shall depend on you, and you alone, to manage the young men."

"I shall not fail you," was all he said, as Salome locked the door of the hall behind them, and they went over the girl's wing to find the others.

The bedrooms on this wing were like those on the other side. There were ample closets and plenty of light and air and window space. The rooms were not spacious, but they were complete in every respect, and a vast improvement on anything the Shawsheen mill girls had ever seen.

"I did not want large rooms," said Salome;

"I think it is better to put not more than two girls in a room. I shall put two single beds in each, and fit up the rooms with everything necessary for comfort ; then I shall insist that the girls keep their own rooms in the best of order. Oh, you'll see what a disciplinarian I shall be ! "

The third floor was entirely given up to bedrooms, the two wings being entirely separated from each other by the upper portion of the hall which extended to the top of the dome. Every part of the building was beautifully finished, well lighted, and planned for general, practical convenience.

"There, if I never do anything else," said Salome, after they had come out of the place, and stood looking back at it, "I shall feel that I have raised a suitable monument to old Newbern Shepard. I believe, if he could have lived until now, that he would have done the same thing himself—only better."

"He couldn't, Miss Shepard," said Villard. "It is absolutely perfect."

"Yes," admitted Burnham, "it is. But do you realize, Miss Shepard, what an elephant you've got on your hands? It's going to be a fearful tax on your mind and strength to keep it up, and to carry out half you've planned."

" Well, what were health and strength given me for?" Salome asked, with the abruptness which sometimes characterized her.

" Most young women find a solution to that question without running an eleemosynary institution," was Burnham's mental comment; but he said nothing.

" I expect to see my happiest days while I have the care of this establishment. I'm sure I never was so happy as I've been for the past six months. Now, I must finish this great house. I shall need all the suggestions and practical aid you can each give me, especially about the libraries and reading-rooms. As to the selection of books, I'm going to begin with a comparative few. Will you two gentlemen come up to the house to-morrow night, prepared to help make out a suitable list?"

" You forget that I have to go to New York to-morrow," said Burnham. " But Villard can go; and I can help afterwards, you know."

" As soon as we get everything in readiness," pursued Salome, " we will have a formal opening. We'll have music and something good to eat, and a little talking, and perhaps a dance to close with." Salome looked wickedly at her aunt, but the latter paid no heed. " Remember your promise, Mr. Villard."

" I shall not be the one to forget it," he answered.

They separated very soon, Salome and her aunt and Marion taking the architect home with them, and Burnham and Villard going back to the mills.

But all through the afternoon, and all through the watches of the night, one sentence repeated itself to John Villard's heart, comforting and helping him, strangely: " I have counted on you from the first."

XIII.

It was Halloween when the new building was formally opened. Up to that time, only a few privileged persons were allowed to enter its sacred portals; but every one connected with the Shawsheen Mills was invited to be present at the opening.

On the hill, back of the mills, stood one hundred new cottages, each costing from fifteen to twenty-five hundred dollars, and all ready for occupancy; but as yet none of the mill-hands had seen the inside of one of them.

It had been a work of no small magnitude to find a suitable matron for the Newbern Shepard Hall. But, finally, the widow of a former physician in Shepardtown, a woman of excellent character and judgment, and with some experience as matron of a young ladies' school, was secured and duly installed in the two pleasant rooms set apart for her in the girls' wing.

John Villard had relieved Salome's mind of another perplexity, by offering to take up permanent quarters for himself in the young men's side; for, although she had felt the necessity of such an arrangement, she had not liked to ask him to give up what she rightly guessed were more congenial apartments in a quiet corner of the town. But he felt that his influence would be needed at the Hall, and that he could do the work which he hoped to do much better, if he were in the midst of the young men whom he wished to interest in many ways. And before Halloween, he was comfortably settled in two rooms at the Hall.

The evening came, clear and cold; such an evening as only the last of October can give. The building was brilliantly lighted from top to bottom, and decorated with flags and evergreen. Outside, Chinese lanterns and bunting lined both sides of the walk up to the main entrance, and helped to give it a holiday air. A band of street-musicians, who happened to be in town, had been engaged and were stationed in front of the building, where their tolerably harmonious strains gave just as much pleasure to the not over-critical audience that was fast assembling, as Thomas' or Seidl's men could have afforded them.

Inside, Salome waited impatiently. Without any premeditated plan, Villard and Burnham placed her and Marion, with Mrs. Soule in the background—for she "declined to be introduced to these persons"—in the center of the library; and forming themselves into a reception committee, they drafted into service a few of the best-appearing young men, who presented every comer to the owner of the mills and her friend. After giving each one a cordial welcome and hand-shake, Salome told them they were free to inspect the new building as they pleased; and, consequently, every mill-hand, accompanied by every other member of his or her family, went critically over the wonderful new building, which seemed to their unaccustomed eyes a structure of unwonted magnificence, and furnished in a most luxurious style.

It had been fitted up inexpensively, but with the utmost good taste. No carpets were on the floors, but American rugs abounded wher-

ever they had seemed necessary. The library
furniture was of plain, substantial oak, like the
heavy woodwork of the room. Throughout
the rest of the house, bedrooms, dining-rooms,
and class-rooms were furnished with strong,
neat, ash furniture. There were a few good
engravings on the walls of the principal rooms,
and the bookcases were about half-filled with
literature of a harmless and interesting, if light
quality. They had all agreed it would not be
best to fill the shelves at first, but to watch the
popular taste and to "leave room for improvement," as Marion said.

The operatives were simply astonished at
what they saw. Some were even yet incredu-
lous, and whispered that they would not be willing nor able to live in such a place; but many
of the girls' eyes brightened as they inspected
their new quarters, and showed a determination,
on the part of their owners, to come in for some
of the good times they saw in store. It is doubtful if even the lowest ones there did not feel a
new self-respect creeping up in their hearts.
Dress may not make the man, but surroundings
often do the woman.

By half-past eight the stream of people

stopped pouring through the big front doors. Everybody had come in, shaken hands with Salome and Marion, and passed along, scattering themselves over the building.

"Now let's get every one into the hall, above," said Salome, "and have a little talking and some music."

It was some little time before the crowd of visitors could be gathered in one place, but after a while the hall was well filled, and the musicians installed in their place. The sound of the band, indoors, proved an effectual summons for the stragglers. For the first time, Salome, on the platform, faced a surging, eager crowd of her own people in Newbern Shepard Hall.

She had wanted one of her two "faithful henchmen" to take the lead to-night; but they had each refused, saying she was better fitted than they; that it was eminently her own affair and not theirs, and that the success of the opening depended on her alone. The last argument was enough, and, much to Mrs. Soule's horror at seeing "Cora de Bourdillon's daughter" in such a plight, Salome presided over her first meeting,—"exactly as if she were one of those 'woman's rights women.'"

When the musicians had finished, Salome stepped forward, and not without some inward quaking, made her first speech.

It was an occasion the Shawsheen Mill hands never forgot. Salome, always well and appropriately dressed, had not slighted them by refusing to appear at her best. She wore a white China silk costume, rightly thinking her young people would be readily reached by the gospel of good clothes. Her gown was simply made, but fitted exquisitely her well-proportioned figure. Neck and wrists were finished with beautiful old point lace, and she did not scorn to wear her grandmother's diamonds.

Her attractive appearance, her cordial and interested manner, and her winning voice had pleaded her cause with the critical operatives before she had uttered a half-dozen sentences. Her sincerity and earnestness went straight to their sensibilities, and, before she had suspected it, every heart in the room was hers.

"My dear friends," she began, "I never made a speech in my life, and cannot now. I never stood on a platform before ; and only my interest in every one of you brings me here to-night. I only want to say that this building, which you see now for the first time, and which I hope will prove a happy home for many of you, is built to my grandfather's memory. Some who are present to-night remember him and love him still, I hope."

Here several gray-haired men in the audience nodded their heads, and one was heard to mutter, " Ay, ay, we do."

"If he had lived, I think everything in the factory would have been different. Your lives would have been different ; and mine, too, perhaps. For one thing, I don't believe you and I would have grown up strangers to each other. You know, by this time, I am sure, that I have a glorious plan for making the Shawsheen Mills the best on earth.

"Not by tearing down mills and building new and more elegant ones ; not alone by making costly improvements ; but by having—and mind, this is the only way it can be done,—by having the best and most conscientious and intelligent class of operatives in this country,— and that will mean, of course, in the world.

Now, you all know I cannot do this alone; every one of you has a part in carrying out this plan of mine. And unless you all agree to help, it will fail. Don't think I want you to do any impossible thing. I only want every one of you to be the best and do the best you possibly can. You and I are going to have some splendid times in the future. We're going to get better acquainted with each other. We are going to become real friends. On your part, you are going to deserve my good opinion and my honest friendship; on my part, I'm going to deserve your confidence and trust and love; and between us we are going to show the people of Massachusetts that a cotton-factory can become something more than a great machine to grind out yards and yards of unbleached sheeting; and that its operatives can become something better and greater than so many smaller wheels in the machinery. We will show that a factory community may be, and is, a prosperous, happy, contented and intelligent people."

Some of the young men could contain themselves no longer, and broke into enthusiastic applause as Salome uttered the last sentiment.

Villard chuckled secretly as he observed that the leaders in it were the heads of the committees in the recent strike.

"I'm so glad you agree with me," said Salome heartily, when the noise had subsided. "Now, I want to tell you about this house. The rooms are all ready for occupancy. I think there are accommodations for all who care to come. You are to leave the old boarding-houses on the corporation, and I shall have them taken down at once. The price of board will remain the same as at the old houses. The reading-rooms are ready, the library is yours, and we shall soon find means of entertainment and work, which will keep us all contented, I hope. Mr. Villard will occupy rooms on this floor, and the matron, whom I will shortly present to you, will be on the girls' wing. There will be but few rules, and those, I trust, not irksome. I cannot imagine that any one will not be willing to obey them. The new houses on the hill are all ready for the families on the corporation to move into. A few of the larger and better houses are to be let at an increased rental ; but most of them will be let at the old rates. We have a plan, by which any

one who wants to, may, after a little, buy a house
and pay for it by monthly installments, just
the same as you pay rent. But I will not go
into details. Mr. Fales will be at the first cottage on the hill, and you can all make arrangements with him at any time after to-morrow
morning. Now I have talked too long, I know,
and am going to stop. I want to have you
hear what Mr. Burnham and Mr. Villard have
to say ; but first we must have some music."

If Salome could have read the trembling
waves of sympathy and reverence which were
already vibrating from the hearts of the young
people whom she had addressed, she would not
have sat down with the feeling of self-distrust
and failure which followed her speech. The
experience, the very atmosphere, was unique in
the history of industrial experiments.

The two superintendents followed the band
with speeches that were characteristic of each.
Burnham's, witty and tinged with sarcasm, but
friendly and cordial enough ; and Villard's,
strong with earnest purpose and full of brotherly love. The matron, Mrs. French, was presented, also, and her few remarks won a
friendly recognition among the young folks ;

and then Salome announced that the meeting would adjourn to the dining-rooms in the basement.

More refined audiences than hers have not been slow to exchange an atmosphere of sentiment and intellectuality for one of prosaic salads and cold meats, and more fanciful ices and coffee ; and the Shawsheen operatives were soon encountering a more æsthetic collation, it is probable, than had ever been served them before. But as it was a bountiful one, they acted well their part and found no fault.

The crowning delight of the evening came afterward. The young men were asked to lend a hand, and soon the floor was cleared in the large hall, and word was circulated through the house that the evening's entertainment would close with dancing. Nothing could have gone so far toward convincing the mill-hands that Salome had meant what she said, than this concession to their social rights, unless it was the fact that she, herself, —the haughty, aristocratic daughter of Floyd Shepard, whom they had looked upon with envy not unmixed with hatred,—that she should lead the dance with the younger superintend-

ent. An orchestra of three pieces was selected
from the band of musicians, and Marion and
Salome, by turns, furnished the piano accompaniment. Salome claimed her promise from
Villard and danced merrily, not only the first
figure but several others. Mrs. Soule was too
much overcome by all she had seen and heard
to endure this, and was taken home ; but the
others staid until the midnight hour tolled, and
the dancers had all bidden good-night to their
newly-developed friends and gone home enthusiastic in their praise of the new order of
things in the mill *régime*, and, especially, of
the woman who was opening to them the wider
doors of opportunity.

11

XIV.

JOHN VILLARD passed a wakeful night in
his new rooms at Newbern Shepard Hall. A
strange and unwonted feeling had taken pos-
session of him; one which he was slow to
recognize, but which cried loudly to him of
his folly and presumption, even while it refused
to be put off.

After that first dance, Salome had paused by
an open window and he had stood idly watching her. Suddenly a tremendous desire to
clasp her in his arms, to hold her close, to
demand her full surrender, swept over him. So
sudden and strong was the passion, that it was
with difficulty that he kept from seizing the
soft hand which lay dangerously near on the
window-sill. So over-mastering was it, that he
dared not stay or even speak. He turned on
his heel and went out under the quiet stars,
alone.

In the days when she had held aloof from the mill, and the superintendents scarcely ever saw her, Geoffrey Burnham had regarded her as " something too bright and good for human nature's daily food," looking upon her as immensely above him, socially speaking. But now that she had become familiarly associated with them in the daily affairs and interests of the mill, Burnham thought of her as having entered the field of good comradeship, and felt that friendly, if not exactly equal, terms existed between them.

With John Villard it was different. He had begun by looking with a certain degree of scorn upon a woman who held tremendous interests so lightly as she had done in the old days. He had felt for her all the contempt a man who does not know them—a man with serious purposes—may feel for the irresponsible butterflies he imagines society-girls to be. With her deeper interest in the side of life which interested him, and her efforts to raise the standard of the mills, her realization of what to him was a sacred object in life and her devotion to it, his thought of her had changed.

With him, familiar every-day contact had not

made of her a comrade, in the ordinary sense of the word. Her beauty and refinement, together with the consciousness which never left his sensitive soul, that it was her wealth and her generosity which made the new conditions possible,—these things only served to raise her to a pedestal where she stood, forever apart from the rest of the universe,—a woman to be revered and worshiped; not a woman to be aspired to.

Suddenly, he found himself in love with her. The tide of feeling which swept over him was one that no man could mistake. It was not enough that he might worship her on her pedestal, with a devotion silent and unknown. He wanted to hold her in his arms. He wanted her eyes to droop before his glance—not to look at him in the steady fashion he knew so well. He wanted to feel her heart beating against his. He wanted to kiss her.

"Poor fool!" he told himself, a hundred times that night. "As if she would even look at me—a poor factory-boy, self-educated, self-trained, and—yes, self-conceited!"

He remembered his youth; how poor he had been; how he had studied by moonlight to save the expense of a candle; how he had worked all through his boyhood in a cotton-mill, that he might help his older sister to support their mother; how, after his mother had died and his sister married, he had remained poor and alone and almost friendless; how little he had seen and known of women; how utterly lacking he was in all the graces of society and the refinements that he supposed to come from outward polish only; in short, how utterly at variance with her tastes and interests and aims his life had been.

He remembered her life of luxury, of travel, of careful training, and the indulgence of cultivated, æsthetic tastes. What was he, that he should dare to even think of her? What but a presumptuous fool, that he should dream of touching even her frail, white hand? And yet, her eyes had drooped when they met his that day, when they all went over the Hall together. Stay—what did it mean? Did she? —could she feel?—but, no. He was a presumptuous idiot to think of it.

He paced the floor for an hour. Then he lit a cigar and, under its peaceful influences, he tried again to fix his mind on the mills, on the

changed condition of things, on anything,—
but her. Still, constantly, over and over, her
tall, white-robed figure took shape in the curl-
ing wreaths of vapor, and he fell to dreaming
what it would be like to have a happy home of
his own, with her as its center and joy.

Again, he was exasperated with himself and
called himself hard names. He threw away the
half-smoked weed and resolutely prepared for
bed; but only to toss wearily about, combat-
ing himself on the old grounds until the dawn,
pushing its way through the crevices of his
blinds, told him to rise and set his face again
toward the workaday world. It was the first
time that hard-working, earnest, practical John
Villard had ever passed a sleepless night.

He had hardly seen how he was to bear the
daily contact with Salome, after that. He was
too modest and too honest with himself to
dream that there might be any hope for him.
He had, at one time during the night, thought
of leaving the mills, and going away to try a
new and easier life than this promised to be.
Then he called himself a coward and remembered her words:

"I have depended on you from the first,"

and he determined to stay, cost what it might. Besides, all his hopes and interests were with the Shawsheen workers. No : he could not leave them, he could not leave her now.

So he went forth in the morning, unchanged in outward appearance, and yet, stronger and better for this first grand fight with himself. And he met her with his usual deferential bow and smile when, by and by, she came to the office for her usual morning's study of business affairs.

It was unanimously agreed that the opening of the Hall had been a grand success. The mill-hands, themselves, seemed to feel the new attitude into which they had suddenly stepped, and were already brighter and more hopeful.

On her way to the mills, Salome had met a young overseer, who was hurrying in to town for something. She greeted him pleasantly, calling him by name, when, to her surprise, he stopped.

"I'd like to thank you, Miss Shepard," the burly young fellow began, "for what you are doing for us. If all the employers took the interest in their operatives as you do in us, we'd want no more Unions, and there'd be no

more strikes. I'm thinking you've got ahead
of the rest of us on the labor question, and
found the right answer to it."

"I'm very glad to hear you say that,"
Salome answered, with a glow at her heart
which no speech from a man of the world had
ever produced. "I want to find it, if I haven't
yet. But, you know it doesn't depend on
me alone. I may try, as hard as I can, but if
you people don't co-operate with me, I'm helpless. I want to depend on you, Mr. Brady."

"And you can that, miss," was the hearty
answer. "You've got us all on your side now,
sure. I went up this morning to see the houses.
They are fine ones, too."

"And did you pick out one for yourself, Mr.
Brady? You are married, I believe?"

"I am that; and I've got as good a wife as
ever the saints sent to bless a man. Yes, I
picked out the one I liked best; but the
woman'll have to see it first, you know. And
then, do you know, I think I'll buy it. The
terms are so easy, and I've a little money laid
by, that I'd like to use; and I'm thinking
Carrie'd be happier in a home of our own."

"Now, that's sensible of you," said Salome,

delighted that her houses were in such good prospect of pleasing. "If you do it, I've no doubt a good many others will. And, by and by, we shall have quite a community of property owners."

Brady straightened himself up unconsciously at the word, touched his hat and passed on, his heart warmed and gratified by the kindly notice ; while Salome entered the office in unusually good spirits.

"It seems to me," she began, addressing herself to Burnham, "that everything is swinging round into the circle of my plans far better than I had dared hope. I expected opposition, or at least indifference, on the part of the operatives. On the contrary, they are all as delighted with the state of affairs as I am."

" Why shouldn't they be ? " was Burnham's comment. " They'd be ungrateful wretches if they weren't. They've far more to gain than you have to lose, remember."

" But you've been trying to make me believe," pursued Salome, " that they didn't want their condition improved ; that they were satisfied to be let alone ; and that they'd resist every improvement I offered."

"Wait a little and see;" Burnham tried to make his tone impartial, if not skeptical; "you've only begun yet. Don't expect the habits of months and years, the loose customs and low tastes, are going to be overthrown in a single night. The affair of last night, for instance, was doubtless the most orderly entertainment and the quietest dance they ever had. But it don't follow that they will all of them be satisfied to drop entirely the old order of low dances when they had plenty to drink, even if they didn't have salads and coffee, or ice-cream and cake. There's no telling how many of them will be stealing off to those places before winter is over."

"Then we must get up some form of entertainment that will hold them to us," said Salome firmly. " They sha'n't fall back, if anything we can compass can save them."

Villard looked across his big ledger at her, as if she had been an angel sent from Heaven direct, to preach a higher political economy to the cotton factories of earth. She caught his look and smiled back at him ; but she said no more.

She did not speak to him until just as she was ready to go home.

"How do you like your new quarters, Mr. Villard?" she said, then. "I hope you rested well last night?"

Villard remembered his sleepless hours vaguely, as in a dream. She looked so bright and untroubled herself.

"You deserted me after that first dance. Did I dance so badly that you feared or dreaded to be caught by me again? If it hadn't been for Mr. Burnham and Mr. Fales I should have felt quite a wall-flower."

"You never could be that, Miss Shepard," poor Villard managed to say.

"Well, as soon as the young people get moved in we must start some classes. I know a good dressmaker whom I can get, and Marion will teach them some other things, if they want it."

She lingered some minutes, talking over the Hall and her plans, and left him with a confused image of herself mixing up with the figures of the ledger in a most incongruous way. Alas! John Villard was to have many a hard fight with himself before he could drive away that image at will.

The young operatives—and all that dwelt within the corporation boarding-house walls—began that very night to pick up their effects, and make ready to move into their new quarters. Mrs. French had all she could attend to in preparing for her large family, assigning rooms, and attending to the thousand details of opening the Hall. But before the week was closed, every old boarding-house was closed and the new home full.

Marion Shaw found her time altogether occupied. Her work was to lie directly among the girls, as Villard's influence was to save the boys and young men. Marion had a gentle and pleasing manner that made friends everywhere she went. She had had a good deal of experience in managing boarding-school girls, and although they are a widely different class from factory girls, human nature—girl-nature, is the same everywhere. Before the week was over, Marion had made friends with many of the girls, and had already interested them in keeping their rooms tidy, in forming a girls' club, which should embrace all sorts of good ends, and in rousing in them what was of infinite value in the work she had laid out,—a desire to become as near like her and Salome as it was possible for them to be.

"We shall have to endure the cross of having them cut all their dresses like ours, wear ribbons like ours, do up their hair like ours, and get up the most astonishing hats purporting to be like ours," said she to Salome one night; "but if it all comes of their wanting to be like us,—you understand me, dear,— I mean of their wanting to reach a higher ideal of course,—we can bear it."

"We shall have to," was the answer. "The truth of it is, they will be trying to copy our habits and manners and characters, too."

"Then we shall have to be all the more careful," said Marion seriously.

Life to Marion Shaw was a serious thing. Although she was but twenty-seven years old, she had come to realize that life may not be for any what the fancy of youth pictures it; and even to realize that the highest good which life can hold is not to be happy. Already she knew that happiness is but a relative term, and that only by ceasing to search and plan for it, can any of us find it even in small degree.

Just now, she walked dangerously near to happiness. On the opening night, Geoffrey Burnham had kept closely at her side all the evening, and after the affair was over, he had walked home with her, while Robert Fales had gone ahead with Salome.

At the door, the two had paused a little, looking at the exquisite, moonlit October night. Suddenly the extraordinary interest Burnham had felt in this young woman had culminated. He seized both her hands in his, and pressed them close to his breast.

"Why have you not come to me before?" he murmured, passionately. "Why have you waited all these years?"

"I was waiting for you," she answered, with a smile.

XV.

ONE evening in January, Salome and Marion went over early to Newbern Shepard Hall. Marion's duties called her there every evening, and she was seldom unaccompanied by her friend.

The success of Salome's schemes for the interest of the working-girls seemed already assured. Although the Hall had been open but little more than two months, classes in dressmaking and millinery and in domestic science were already established, and were well attended. Some girls there were, it is true, who felt that, after working all day, they were entitled to an idle evening, or to the right of amusing themselves after their own fashion. But plenty of young women had been found to open the classes, and the number was steadily increasing. No strong measures had been

taken to induce these girls to join. Marion
had talked with some of them individually, at
first, and found a few who, half skeptically,
had consented to try the dressmaking class, as
an experiment. Then the announcement was
made that a class would be opened on a certain night, and twenty-six girls were present.
Instruction in sewing, cutting and fitting was
given free to any woman connected with the
Shawsheen Mills. As the girls had been paying exorbitant prices for having cheap material
poorly made up, and as Salome had provided
instructors from the best dressmaking establishment Shepardtown afforded, the girls were
not slow to see the benefit that would come to
them.

The young wives of operatives, too, women
with houses and children to care for, then
began to avail themselves of the privileges
which the class afforded. So that, on this January evening, there were over a hundred and
fifty women in the classes, and another room
had been opened to them on the ground
floor.

It was the same with other classes. At first,
the young women had joined with the older

ones in " pooh-poohing " the cooking and
housekeeping lectures and demonstrations.
The idea that they and their mothers did not
know how to cook, and that Salome, who knew
absolutely nothing of such matters, essayed to
teach them, was a most distasteful one. But
when they found that a celebrated teacher was
to come out twice a week from Boston, and give
demonstrations in the model class-rooms below,
and that a graduate of the Boston Cooking
School had been engaged to take charge of
the lessons every evening, they, the young
married women from the cottages, especially,
dropped in from curiosity ; and although they
had come to scoff, they remained to cook. In
short, they had become deeply interested in the
new ways of housekeeping, and were surprised
and delighted to find a way of making their
few dollars go farther and procure a better and
more healthful living. Consequently, these
classes, too, were full, although the older
matrons did not yet give up their prejudices.

Among the girls who had not yet joined the
classes, there were many who sat quietly in
their own rooms or in the large reading-rooms,
and enjoyed the current magazines and papers,

or gossiped quietly and harmlessly about the fashions and each other—not altogether unlike women of higher pretensions. It was astonishing, even to Salome, who had, from the first, believed in her girls, how few of them went out on the streets at night.

"It is not astonishing to me," said Marion, that January evening, in reply to a remark from her friend to this effect. " The girls are tired at night and are only too glad to have a pleasant, light and steam-heated place to stay in. Their rooms at the old boarding-houses were cold, barren and dismal. In winter weather they could not sit in them, and the so-called parlor was not much better. When I was at Mme. Blanc's one of her servant girls went wrong. I shall never forget something she said. When Madame heard of it, she sent for the girl and asked her, bitterly, what had made her bring such a scandalous thing upon a select house like hers. I was in her room at the time. The poor girl looked up at Mme. Blanc and said, ' O, ma'am, you're awful particular about where your young ladies spend their evenings,—girls that you're paid for looking after. But us servant girls— how did you look after us ? You didn't allow us a light in our own rooms, or to speak above a whisper in the kitchen, or seem to think we was human beings at all. What else could we do, but go out on the street when we wanted a bit of freedom? And once, on the street, ma'am, girls like us ain't never safe. If you'd looked out for me, ma'am, and treated me as well as you treat your own dog or cat, it would never have happened.' Poor Madame was overcome entirely, and the girl left her white with rage. But she looked after her servants more closely afterward, and kept them in at night in warm rooms. I don't believe our girls want to do wrong,—especially if we make it comfortable for them to do right."

On the young men's side, things had gone equally well. There was a class of them who, like their fathers before them, were sturdy, honest and faithful. It was a small class, but upon these John Villard depended to counteract the influence of the lower foreign element that had crept in ; and to the pride of these he appealed, both directly and indirectly, in his efforts to establish a better social atmosphere among the operatives.

With a few of these to begin with, he had

opened an evening school on the other wing of
the Hall; and, as in the case of the women's
classes, it had increased in numbers and interest
from the start. The overseers, almost to a
man, gladly availed themselves of its opportunities for the education that the true American
always feels the need for; and they, with the
better class of men from the looms and mules,
set the example for others to follow.

No better man for the work could have been
chosen than John Villard. He had come up
under much the same conditions that governed
them. He had begun on the lowest round,
and worked up to the position he now occupied,
by hard work and the closest application to
business. This fact, together with his attitude
toward them during the strike, had made him
a favorite with nearly every man on the works.
They felt that they could place the utmost
confidence in Villard; and in the Shawsheen
Mills, as everywhere, a rugged sincerity and
honesty of purpose carried a weight that even
the most unstable felt.

The lecture-hall was usually packed at the
weekly entertainment which Salome provided,
and a new feeling of content and self-respect

had begun to permeate the mills. Make a
man who has been looked upon as a mere
machine feel that he is estimated at something
near the worth which every human being feels
in his heart that he is entitled to, and you have
done much to raise him to a higher social
standard. For the first time since old Newbern
Shepard's day, the mill-hands began to feel
a just pride in being individual American
citizens. Unconsciously, both men and women
were setting their faces toward the higher
standards which Villard by his life, and
Salome by her newly awakened energy, had
set for them.

At the mills, affairs were on a most flourishing basis. The Shawsheen brand of cloth was
too well known to allow of a few months shut-
down of the mills making any difference in the
law of demand. Orders had increased, even
while the mills were closed, and they had been
worked to their utmost capacity ever since they
had opened. Never had the Shawsheen Mills
been more prosperous than at the beginning of
January, or their future looked brighter.

When Villard had opened his evening school
he invited Burnham to co-operate with him;

but the latter had put him off without a definite reply, and not until the afternoon of the day referred to in the beginning of this chapter had Villard asked him whether or not he might count on his assistance. Burnham occasionally looked in at the Hall of an evening, but Villard had begun to suspect that this was principally for the purpose of seeing Marion Shaw.

"Well, to tell the truth," Burnham finally admitted, "I've no taste for this sort of thing. Oh, yes; it's a good scheme, and seems to be working first-rate; but I'm not the right fellow for the place. I don't like philanthropic work, never did, never shall. I work hard enough during the day. I need rest and freedom at night."

Villard smiled.

"And I suppose I don't do anything day-times and need this sort of thing as recreation and intellectual stimulus?" His tone was sarcastic, for he had little patience with selfishness in any form.

"No, not that," said Burnham. "You work hard enough—too hard, in fact. But all this is more in your line. You're like Miss

Shepard; you're both of you happier working yourselves to death for others. Now, I'm not built on that plan. I've no faculty for teaching, and I'm sure that my well-meant efforts to meet the men half-way are looked upon by them as condescension on my part."

He waited an instant for Villard to speak, but no answer came.

"I can't help it. I wasn't born to the manor, so to speak. I didn't come up from the ranks, as you know. I suppose they'd believe in me more, if I had. But you know that my father put me under Mr. Greenough to learn the business, only after I had graduated from college and fooled away a year in Europe. I sometimes doubt if I'm not out of place in this mill as it is run nowadays."

"Oh, no, not that," put in Villard hastily. "You're too good a business man. We couldn't spare you."

"I can see how it's all coming out," Burnham continued, as if he had not heard Villard. "You two" (Villard's heart jumped at the words) "will go on and make a model institution of the Shawsheen Mills. I should doubt if you made a profitable one, only that I know you've got a mighty good business head on your shoulders ; and, I say, the way Miss Shepard is developing is a caution to us men. I'd no idea she'd take such a practical turn, or learn the details so readily. Oh, I can see where it's going to end. She'll be the recognized head and you'll be her first assistant. As for me, I sha'n't be in it. I shall have resigned."

"Jeff !" It was only occasionally that these two called each other by their boyhood names.

" Yes, I don't think I should care to have it known that I worked under a woman, much as I admire and respect Miss Shepard. There'd be no other way, unless I married her ! "

Villard turned pale with sudden, inward rage, but he said nothing.

" Don't think I'd have much chance there, though," Burnham went on lightly. " You're more her style. And you're both so much wrapped up in good works that you've no time for faith in each other, beyond what you waste in philanthropic effort. Miss Shepard don't seem to be the marrying kind. I don't believe she ever thinks of a man unless he has the merit of being an operative in the mills."

" And since you're bent on discussing matrimonial matters," observed Villard, with sarcasm, " how about Miss Shaw ? And when are the wedding-cards to be issued ? "

Burnham shook the ashes from his cigar and looked at his watch critically.

" Marion Shaw is a fine girl," he said. " She's the right kind of woman to tie to; but "—and Burnham took up his hat to go out—" I'm not the marrying kind either."

So Villard had come to understand that he must take care of his evening school as best he could alone.

Robert Fales had settled in Shepardtown. There were to be more cottages built in the spring, and to him Salome had alone confided her plan of erecting a new church which should be named for her grandfather. When the evening school began to grow, he went to Villard and offered his services as assistant, and had proved a most valuable one.

This evening Salome looked in upon them, and asked Villard if he could give her a few moments after the class.

" I shall be very glad," he replied. " I have been working up the idea you spoke about the other day, and wanted to talk with you about it."

"The profit-sharing scheme?" asked Salome. "That's just what I wanted to speak of. It seems to me we ought, now, at the beginning of the year, to get it into manageable shape, and tell the men, so that they may know what to expect. I will be in the reception-room when your class is through."

Much as Villard was interested in his work the remaining hour dragged a little. The prospect of a quiet *tête-à-tête* with Salome, even on so unromantic a subject as profit-sharing, was too alluring.

But, at last, he found himself face to face with her, and for a few moments forgot all else in the pleasure of listening to her voice and watching the curve of her chin and mobile lips, as she talked of immaterial things.

"And now, what kind of a plan have you formulated as to the profit-sharing?" she asked, after a little.

"Profits—oh, yes," said Villard, suddenly brought to himself. "I have examined all the accounts of such experiments in foreign countries, and tried to remember the differing conditions and better wages here. I have prepared a rough draft of a circular which I thought perhaps you might like to send out among the hands. Do you want to see it?"

"Of course," was the answer.

"I don't pretend it is complete, you know," he went on, drawing a folded paper from his inner pocket. "It is only an abstract, but—here it is."

"Read it to me, please," said Salome.

He would rather have had her read it, while he watched her face; but he complied.

"For some time past," the circular read, "the subject of co-operation in some form has been considered by the Shawsheen Mills. Believing that capital and labor are interdependent and their interests identical, it has been decided to adopt some plan by which the laborer may obtain a share of the product in proportion to the profits of the scheme, at the same time guaranteeing his wages against the time of loss.

"It is now proposed, therefore, to divide a sum among the Shawsheen employes, each year in which there are surplus profits, over and above wages earned.

"Understand, that before anything can be set apart for this purpose, wages must be paid, interest must be paid, and a fair profit on capital must be paid. In addition to this, an additional amount must be set aside to make good the wear and tear of buildings and machinery, and to strengthen reserve funds against a time of depression.

" Ordinarily, the sum above all these amounts must be small, and must differ, of course, with the fluctuations of the market, the depression of trade, and the wear of machinery from year to year. It will be readily seen, also, that the sum to be divided will be enlarged by extra care and attention on the part of employes. Every weaver who makes a mis-pick, every burler who slights her work, every spinner who makes a needless knot; in short, every person who makes an unnecessary waste of any kind, makes the amount to be divided smaller, by making a loss to the concern; and, on the other hand, if every person in the mill attends to the little savings, the wool-washers saving every scrap of wool, the spinners making less waste, the weavers weaving up the whole bobbin, and so on through all the branches, a great saving can be made which will effectually increase the sum to be divided; and it will be for the direct interest of every employe to exercise such increased care and diligence.

"The mode of distributing this bonus will be by making a dividend of so much per cent. upon the wages earned by each person. If, after all contingencies are provided for, there is not enough left to make a dividend of one per cent., no dividend will be made for that year. In case of a dividend it will be paid on and after the first day of May in each year to all employes who have been in employ at the Shawsheen Mills for at least seven months during the year, and shall .not have been discharged for drunken or disorderly conduct. The amount of wages earned during the year preceding the first of April shall be the amount upon which the bonus for each individual shall be computed.

"The profit for the present year, if there be a dividend, will be paid on or after the first day of May. Let every person connected with the mills work so faithfully, making every effort toward a wise economy, that the first dividend shall be an encouraging one."

John Villard stopped reading the circular and looked across at Salome. She was regarding him with a fixed look of admiration and reverence, such as a good woman feels for but one man in a lifetime. For an instant his pulses leaped ; but he was too modest a man to believe in his own good fortune.

" Well, what do you think of it ? " he asked.

His words brought her to herself. Her expression faded to one of mere brightness, and became less frankly honest.

" I think it capital," she said. " I do not see how it can be improved. Will you let me take it home and consider it ? "

" Of course," he assented. " You know I do not pretend it is perfect. But it seems to me we risk nothing in trying it."

Salome rose to go and reached out her hand for the manuscript. Some pieces had fallen on the table and in gathering them up, their hands brushed against each other.

An electric thrill shot through the frame of each. Salome stood, blushing and sweet, suddenly conscious that a crucial moment in her life had come. Had Villard but spoken, had he but clasped the hand that still remained near his !

But, ever depreciating himself and knowing absolutely nothing of the heart of woman, he turned abruptly away, bringing Salome back to herself with a hasty " good-evening." And then he strode away to the outer air, asking himself, savagely, why he was so weak and boyish because a pretty woman happened to touch his hand.

XVI.

ALL through the winter months, Geoffrey Burnham and Marion Shaw were constantly meeting. As Burnham had intimated to Villard, he had taken only a superficial interest in the philanthropic or ethical side of mill-economy. But he was often at the Hall of an evening; and upon pleasant nights, when the ladies walked over from the Shepard mansion, he accompanied them home after the evening's engagement. If it were early, as on ordinary occasions, he went in and sat chatting with them for an hour or two. Mrs. Soule always welcomed him, and although she never went to the Hall, she found ample opportunities of telling him how many lonely hours it caused her.

"I often wish Salome cared half as much," she used plaintively to say on these occasions, "for a living aunt as for a dead grandfather."

Often, Burnham sang to Salome's accompaniment, his rich tenor voice lending pathos, and his ardent glances a meaning, for Marion in the love-songs he sang so well. The latter sat silent at such times, a quiet content wrapping her round, forgetting the past, ignoring the future.

" A blind man's paradise," she told herself it was, as the weeks rolled by, and the glamour of a scarcely hinted but very evident passion waited in vain for more than the vaguest expression.

Sometimes the two were left alone for a while, when the conversation took a fitful tone, as if uncertain whether to be light and frivolous, or tender and deep. Several times Burnham had seized Marion's unresisting hand and kissed it passionately ; and, finally, one evening when they were alone, he had put his arm about her waist and drawn her close to him.

" Why have we not had each other all these years ? " he asked, looking into her sweet, confused eyes. " What cruel fate has kept you from me ? "

" It does not matter, does it, so long as we have each other now ? " Marion had asked in reply. And then he had bent and kissed the pure white brow and the clustering rings of hair.

After this, every night, Marion, kneeling by her bedside alone, thanked God for the love that had come to brighten her bereaved life.

And Burnham? Did he realize what he might be doing when he won this true and loyal woman's heart? At first, he, too, was happy in the present. The past held nothing which he was proud to remember; and into the future he stubbornly refused to look. He had, for years,—" since his days of adolescence," he told himself,—had no interest in women, although he knew that, in a place like Shepardtown, he was the object of several fond mammas' machinations, and the admiration of most of the village girls. He had never met Marion's counterpart. She interested and fascinated him. Simple and childish in many ways, she was grave and dignified in others. Her life, he could see, would be spent for others. She was one of those women who are a constant sacrifice to the world around them ; who give openly and always of their best, asking and expecting little in return. In short—

Burnham knew it as well as any one could—
she was a woman whose life and love and
utmost service would be absorbed by a selfish
man, only to be as unappreciated as they were
undeserved on his part. And yet, ever since
their first meeting, months before, there had
been that subtle consciousness of each other
drawing them on, that wave of feeling on
meeting, that positive yearning when they were
separated.

After Villard's pointed questioning regarding Marion, Burnham began to question himself seriously. At first, when thoughts of the
future had intruded into his calm moments, he
thought of her as his wife ; of himself as settled
down in a house of his own.; he even expected
to be happy. But he did not put his thoughts
into words. When he was with Marion, he
avoided—not so much from intention perhaps
as from a reluctance to break the spell of romance which hung over them—any mention
of different relations in the future.

It was April before he brought himself to
face about and look at the subject, calmly and
seriously. Just where was he drifting with
Marion ?

One day he allowed himself to let fall some remark about her to Villard,—not in any way implying their peculiar relations, but yet speaking of her in such a way that Villard drew himself up to his straightest, and looked him in the the eye a full moment. Not a word was said, but at that instant, Burnham felt the disagreeable consciousness of being a scoundrel.

He went home that evening and tried to read. Then he tried to smoke. Then he thought of going over to the Shepard mansion. He finally decided on sitting down and squarely meeting an issue that should have been faced six months before.

Geoffrey Burnham was thirty-seven years old. He had considered only his own taste and desires ever since he was born. When he was a boy, if he had wanted anything, he had it. If his father did not grant his every wish his mother would. And she, poor woman, had fostered in him the idea that all his personal, imperious desires were meant, always, to be immediately granted. The conquering of Self had been no part of his early discipline.

His father died when he was in Europe. When he came home, and entered the mills,—an arrangement the father effected just before his decease,—his pretty, white-faced mother had come to Shepardtown to be near her son. For him she lived and would die. Yielding weakly in everything to him, she avenged her position by setting herself against all other women. Salome had called upon her, and had invited her to her house, but in vain. Mrs. Burnham went nowhere, and wanted to see no one. Her son was all in all to her. And but for the constant fear that he would marry the handsome Miss Shepard, who, with all her wealth, she felt sure, would crowd her completely out of her son's heart and home, she would have been a comparatively happy woman. Incredible to larger-hearted women, as it seems, there are women so selfish in their devotion to an only son, as to wreck his life, so far as its being of any practical value to himself and others is concerned, by the strength of their own weak persistence.

Burnham thought of his mother. He remembered the comfortable habits he had settled into; he wondered if any other woman would ever let him smoke in the best room in the house, or submit to his will when he chose, as he often did for days together, to speak only in monosyllables in his own house. He felt that, should he marry, his habits would all have to be changed; that the solitude which he prized, when he felt so inclined, might be absolute no longer. He remembered his mother's peculiarities, and said to himself that there would be a devil of a row, should he undertake to bring a wife home. There might be constant bickerings, and that he never could abide. No; better let women alone.

Then he thought of Marion and sighed. Her tender eyes, when he parted from her two nights before, came up before him.

"Hang it," he asked himself; "just how far have I gone with her, anyway?"

He felt himself a scoundrel again, to his credit be it written. But then, there were the habits of a lifetime, and his mother to be remembered. Could he overthrow all his established convictions?

And yet, just what might Marion be expecting of him? No, he had given her no definite encouragement in words. Still, one never can tell how a good, pure woman is going to take these things.

Burnham went out under the April sky and walked up and down the concrete walk bareheaded, until his mother, from her window, reminded him for the third time that he would certainly get cold out there; and shouldn't she make him a cup of hot negus? Then he came in and renewed the conflict.

"I've let the thing run too long," he said to himself, as he gazed into the open wood-fire, having refused the decoction his mother had patiently brought him. "I'll have a reckoning with myself to-night, and decide this thing once for all."

Burnham was a decided man, and, once determined, seldom changed his mind. He boasted, sometimes, of that quality, forgetting that it is only an ignorant or an unprogressive soul which will never acknowledge itself in the wrong, or change its course from the one marked out, perhaps in obstinacy or error.

Until midnight he argued with himself, although, unconsciously, his mind had been secretly made up at the start. When the clock struck twelve he rose and got together his writing materials.

He had fully decided that it would be folly

for him to marry Marion Shaw. She was a rarely devoted, unselfish woman, and a most lovable one; but he knew himself, he said, and if she married him she would do so only to be unhappy in the end. She could not be otherwise, living with him and his mother.

But how was he to withdraw from the delicate situation in which he had foolishly placed himself? There was, he decided, but one way.

For a year, now, Salome Shepard had been making a deep and practical study of the mills and their operation. She had proved a wonderfully apt scholar, her womanly intuition often grasping, in a few minutes, details which he had been months in learning. He doubted if, should occasion require it, she could not run the mills alone. With Villard—honest, faithful soul!—to help her, Burnham felt that there was no longer any need of his services at the Shawsheen Mills. There was another superintendency in a mill at Lowell which stood open to him, whenever he chose to take it. There were some things about it that he would not like; but he must not remain on dangerous ground. He took great credit to himself as he reflected that honor required him not to trifle with Marion's feelings another day. He virtuously decided to take himself out of her way. Once gone from her she would cease to feel his attraction and forget the tender scenes between them. He would resign his connection with the Shawsheen Mills.

He sat down and wrote the letter of resignation. Then he went to bed and slept. He, like Villard, had kept awake hours for a woman. But he was not the man to conquer his selfish nature, or to grow stronger by fighting himself.

* * * * * * * *

The next morning Salome found Villard alone in the inner office of the mills. A note lay on her desk. It was Burnham's resignation.

She uttered an exclamation of surprise, and turned to Villard.

"Did you know about this?" she asked, handing him the note.

Villard looked as astonished as though a dynamite bomb had exploded in the mill-yard.

"Not a word," he said. "But stay, he did hint at something, months ago; but I never gave it a second thought. 'Decided that he is no longer needed on the works, and an opportunity having offered to better his condition.' H'm! Those are his reasons? Strange he hadn't mentioned the matter to me although it *was* his own business."

"But what are we going to do? Can't we get him back?" asked Salome.

"We can try," was the reply, "but Burnham is a pretty determined fellow when he fairly makes up his mind. Shall I go over and see him?"

"If you please. Tell him to come back with you; I want to persuade him to stay if I can."

Villard went over to Burnham's house, but he had already gone to Lowell to complete arrangements to enter the new position. Mrs. Burnham knew nothing of either this plan or her son's sudden resignation. Villard returned to Salome.

"What are we going to do," she asked, "supposing he refuses to come back—even at an increased salary?"

"Don't you think you and I can run the business alone for a while?" returned Villard, "at least until we can find a good man. Good superintendents don't grow on every bush."

" Do you think I am capable of taking his place—with your help, of course ? " Salome looked earnestly at him.

" I think you are quite capable of doing anything noble and great," he answered, fervently.

" With your help," she said, in a low tone. " Of course I will do anything, and shall be only too proud," she hastened to add, " if I have succeeded in learning enough of the business to be of any use."

Villard looked again at her averted eyes, and checked an impulse to say something more. Had he known a tenth as much of women as of cotton factories, his fortune and happiness had been in his own hands. But he honestly thought she had turned away her eyes and spoken the last sentence to turn him away from saying more ; while she was saying to herself as she turned to her desk again :

" Will he never, never speak ? It will come, some time, I am sure, but will he never dare ? "

XVII.

Burnham returned to Shepardtown only to tell his mother that he should go to Lowell immediately. He had accepted the standing offer there, and expected to begin at once.

In vain Salome offered him an increase of salary. And as he was evidently bent on going, she would not urge him to remain in her employ. But both she and Villard could assign but one reason for his sudden determination. Both felt sure that he had offered himself to Marion and that she had refused him.

Intimate as Salome and Marion were, no discussion of love-matters ever entered their conversation. With each, love was too high and sacred a thing to be bruited about, even in a conversation between friends. In their younger days, when Marion had shyly announced her engagement to a young law-

student, there had been no silly or sentimental
waste of words between them on the subject.
And now, perhaps because both women felt
the stirrings of a deep passion in their inmost
heart, no reference to the subject was ever
made.

When Salome went home to lunch, she told
Marion of Burnham's resignation; but beyond
a momentary look of blank astonishment
Marion's face gave no sign. And Salome's
feeling for her friend was too deep and too
delicate, to ask for what she did not choose to
tell voluntarily.

Burnham would have been glad to leave
town without risking himself in Marion's
presence again.

He feared to trust himself with her, in the
presence of the strange attraction she had held
for him. But common courtesy demanded
that he should call at the Mansion to leave
his good-byes.

Marion heard the news of his resignation
with a strange sinking of the heart. Something told her that this was the end of her
foolish, happy dream. And although she
loyally refused to acknowledge her doubts,

the strange presaging which was something more than presentiment lurked in her heart all day, and kept her uneasy and restless. She half expected Burnham to come in and by a few words settle the question of their relations. She even asked herself, how she could best leave Shepardtown if he insisted upon taking her to Lowell.

But he did not come until evening. Then it happened, as events will in this strange world, that she was with her classes at the Hall. Salome was unusually tired that evening and had remained quietly at home. Burnham dropped in about eight o'clock, sat for half an hour with her and Mrs. Soule, and then bade them good-bye, leaving his adieu for Marion. He did not go to the Hall, although she half expected him all through the long evening. The next morning he took an early train for Lowell.

When Marion came home she heard in amazement that Burnham had been there and gone. Salome gave her his word of parting.

"And was that all?" Marion asked, with strained voice and blazing cheeks.

"That was all. Tell me, dear," asked

Salome, for the first time, "was there any trouble between you? Had you anything to do with his going?"

"No, nothing," and Marion was gone to her room.

On the first day of May, the experiment of profit-sharing was put into effect for the first time at the Shawsheen Mills. In spite of the strike, and the enforced idleness of several months which had followed, previous to the year just passed, this had been a successful one, and when the divisions for capital, machinery and re-serve fund had been set aside, there still remained a surplus which gave a dividend of four and a half per cent. In some cases, this dividend on wages made a very considerable sum, and in all cases the operatives felt a new sensation of direct responsibility and connection with the mills. Besides the addition of this money to their wages, the feeling of brotherhood and ownership it engendered was, Villard declared, quite worth the experiment.

Another circular was sent out, urging the operatives to increased care in saving and painstaking in order that the dividend might be larger another year. And the good results

of the plan were directly manifest in the work
of nearly every employe.

A little incident which occurred soon after
this did much to convince the men of the
changed relations in which they now stood
towards their employers.

An overseer had been tyrannizing over the
spinners until they would endure it no longer.
In Mr. Greenough's day, it is more than probable that the matter would have culminated in
a lock-out or a strike.

But with the new order of things came a
greater feeling of confidence in Villard. Five
of the spinners, therefore, with the consent
of the others, went personally to the superintendent.

After hearing their story, Villard promised
to settle their grievance, and quite a discussion of economic questions concerning Capital
versus Labor followed.

" You men have labor to sell," said Villard,
"and we buy it. We have the products of
your labor to sell, and the commission mer-
chants and others buy it. As much courtesy
and fair dealing should exist between us, as I
like to have between us and the men to whom

we sell. We would not take insolence from a
broker's clerk; you need not put up with the
tyranny of an overseer."

These words, repeated to the other employes,
were the most powerful preventive against
strikes ever tried in the Shawsheen Mills.

As the summer advanced, other new cottages
were built on the hill to accommodate the
growing demand from the operatives. All
those built the previous year were occupied,
and many of them had been bought on the
installment plan. Although the community
around the Shawsheen factories, as it now
existed, had come suddenly into its new rela-
tion, it already represented almost an ideal one.
It was already a practical lesson in social
economics, which many a reformer and many a
capitalist would do well to study. To be a
capitalist even in a small way is to learn to
respect capital. The fact that these men
owned their small plots of ground and their
cottages (even if they were mortgaged for the
greater part of their value) was already digni-
fying the laborer by the tangible proof of his
own value.

By this time, Salome had come to know

14

every family who were in the employ of the mills. Was there trouble coming to any household, was there sickness, was there affliction among them, they all turned to her for help and sympathy, encouragement or congratulation. The smallest events—the birth of a baby, the progress of measles, the love affairs of the young, the querulous complaints of the old—were all of interest to her; and they, in return, appreciated her kindness and returned it with a loyalty of service that did her soul good.

Salome often declared, laughingly, that her relations to them were truly patriarchal. An atmosphere of content and friendliness prevailed where there had been jealousy and bickering.

The popular entertainments were kept up during the summer. There were concerts, at which local talent (often some operative who possessed the faculty of singing a song) appeared. Salome, herself, often presided at the piano, and Marion frequently lent her voice; their theory being that young people who took little or no vacation in summer needed some sort of recreation in summer as in winter.

Towards the close of the summer, as Salome came out of the Hall one evening, one of the young men came up to her side, and asked if he might speak to her alone.

"Certainly," she said; "Mr. Fales, will you walk ahead with Marion, while O'Donovan walks home with me?"

She remembered the young fellow perfectly. She had seen him first during the strike, a handsome young dare-devil who seemed, in fact, to be one of the ringleaders among the younger men. When the mills had re-opened, she had taken an uncommon interest in him. He was a faithful and industrious man, and when, after a few weeks of sneering at the " new-fangled notions," he had settled into harmony with the strange atmosphere, he had tried to improve himself in many ways. When Villard took charge of the evening school, he had held aloof for a few weeks, but at last joined one of Fales' classes. In their entertainments and dances, he had taken leading parts; and that day, Villard had offered him the post of overseer in one of the minor departments at the mills. It was quite a step up for the young man, and Villard had been surprised at his hesitation in accepting the offer.

Salome knew all this; and as she heartily liked the fellow, she determined to influence him for his own interest.

O'Donovan was silent for some moments, after they started, doubtless being unaccustomed to escort ladies of her degree in that friendly way. But Salome soon put him at his ease by her kind and easy manner.

" And so you're going to be promoted," she said, after a little. " I hope you like that ? "

" Miss Shepard," he blurted out in confused speech, " that's what I want to talk about. There's something—I mean, I want to tell—I *ought* to tell you something, Miss Shepard."

" Very well. It oughtn't to be very difficult to do that," and her tone was cordial and encouraging.

" I don't think I ought to take the position —unless you say so. But I expect you'll put me in irons, if I tell you. Only—well, the other fellows would say I was a blasted fool— barrin' your presence, miss."

" Why, John," exclaimed Salome wonderingly. For the young man was in a great

state of excitement. "What can it be?
Surely, you know you need not be afraid of
me?"

"You remember the night some one tried
to blow up the mill—and Mr. Greenough—and
Mr. Villard——" Salome stood still and gazed
through the summer moonlight at her strange
escort. He did not look up, but stood like a
culprit before her.

"I don't know how you managed to find
out and save 'em," he went on. "Miss
Shepard—it was me."

"You? John O'Donovan!" For an instant
there was silence.

"Go on," she said, when she could command her voice. "Tell me all."

"It was John Ross that planned it and put
me up to it. When he died, I wondered if he
hadn't told you or Mr. Villard. Ever since
then, I've been trying to, but somehow I
couldn't—tell Mr. Villard—nor you neither.—
It was John Ross that planned it. He called
me a coward and a scab—and, finally, well
—you know I was a crazy fool then, with the
rest of 'em.—It ain't no use talkin', miss, but
we all discussed and brooded over things until

we were half out of our heads. If any one of us had weakened first, we'd all give up, and the strike would have bu'st; but—well, 'tain't no use talkin', I s'pose. I've confessed, and you can have me put in irons, if you want to."

"How did you come to want to tell me, John?" Salome said softly.

"Oh, miss, when I found how you saved the mill that night, and the lives of those two men, I went down on my knees with thankfulness. It somehow seemed to open my eyes to where I'd been standin'. Then, when the mills opened and you took us back, and when you commenced to take an interest in us; when you built that beautiful big Hall, and all them cottages; and, if you'll pardon me for sayin' it, when you begun walkin' thro' the mills yourself, speakin' a pleasant word to us all and smilin' at us as if we were all your equals, miss—and you a saint,——it was then I seemed no better'n a murderer. And when John Ross died, and the detectives gave up lookin' for the men, it was bore in on me as how I ought to confess; and to-day, when Mr. Villard called me into the office and praised my work, and said I'd been faithful and trust-

worthy——*trustworthy*, ma'am !—why, then,
I couldn't stand it no longer."

The young man stood silent in the moonlight. Salome's eyes were filled with tears.

" John," she said, " you are a noble fellow.
It is no more than right that you should confess this to me, but not all fellows in your place
could do it. You can because you have the
making of a man in you."

The young man looked up.

" And what are you goin' to do with me ? "
he asked.

" Will you do just what I say ? " returned
Salome.

" I will, indeed," he said.

" Then I want you to go to Mr. Villard to-
morrow morning and tell him you accept the
place. Then do your best, and deserve better
things in future."

" Miss Shepard ! " Young O'Donovan fairly
gasped.

" John," she went on, and she seemed to him
like the pictures of saints in the church, as she
stood in her white gown in the silvery light,
" if your scheme had succeeded, you would not
only have destroyed most valuable property of

mine ; you would have killed two of my dearest friends ; but you have turned over a new leaf. I feel sure that nothing will ever induce you to consent to anything of the kind again."

" Never, so help me Heaven ! " he exclaimed, fervently.

" Now, you have confessed like a man, I will forgive like a woman. You will accept the new place. You will go on studying and improving yourself, and some day I shall be proud of you, and you will be proud that you once had the manliness to come to me and confess a crime. Now, we will bury the thing forever, and never speak of it again. Only promise me you will go to Mr. Villard in the morning and do as I ask you."

" I promise," said the young man solemnly. Then he dropped on his knees and seizing her hand, bent his head reverently upon it.

" If the God in Heaven above is like you," he said, " He is a God worth serving."

" My poor forgiveness resembles His, John, only as a drop of rain resembles the mighty ocean."

They walked silently home, and O'Donovan left her with a new purpose in his heart that has never left it since. He is to-day a thriving Christian gentleman. Dare any one say it would have been better to condemn him as a law-breaker?

"Nobody but a woman, I suppose, would have dealt justice so," said Salome to herself, as she put out her light an hour later, and turned to the window—"nobody but John Villard."

XVIII.

A YEAR rolled by—a year of prosperity to
the Shawsheen Mills, and of growth and improvement in the condition of their operatives.
John Villard had been made first superintendent and a new man had taken his place.
Salome continued to act as her own agent and
had developed a keen love and tact for the
business,—a condition of affairs which Mrs.
Soule never ceased to bemoan.

The young people at the Hall were more than
ever the dearest objects of her solicitude. In
most cases, their elevation had been steady and
substantial. Young men had become self-re-
specting and carried themselves with increased
dignity. Young women gradually grew less
frivolous and more earnest. Thrown together
under so much better conditions than formerly,
both sexes emulated the politeness which they

were quick to notice between Villard and Salome. They became more quiet and decorous; they read a better class of books; they began, in their way, to cultivate higher tastes than had been known in the old factory boarding-house or among the tumble-down tenement houses. Several marriages had taken place, at which Salome had acted as the girl's guardian, giving away the bride. Young O'Donovan's was the first of these. His increased pay as overseer enabled him to marry Kitty Kendall, to whom he had long been devoted; and the young bridegroom was even happier than the bride when Salome offered to act in that capacity. Neither of them would have dared ask it of her, but her evident willingness to act on this occasion encouraged those who came after, until Salome said she felt all the responsibilities of a mother with a large family of daughters.

As Villard saw all this marrying and giving in marriage, he grew, at times, more restless. There were occasions when he came suddenly upon Salome, or, perhaps during their rare talks together, when he felt sure for a moment that she felt for him more than a friendly interest. But, remembering his comparative poverty, he never spoke the one word which would have broken down all barriers. And Salome successfully concealed her feeling for him, not daring, even, to examine it herself. So they had drifted on, more than friends and less than lovers, through another year.

There came, at last, the first period of absence from each other since Mr. Greenough's death. Daily association, pleasant as it is, cannot teach lovers how much they love, as can a short separation.

The second dividend of the mills had been declared, each operative getting three and a half per cent., this time, on their wages. When the work consequent on this transaction was closed up, it was decided to put new machinery in the lower mills. There was an improved kind in one of the Holyoke mills, and it was decided that Villard should go, personally, to examine its workings, leaving Salome and the second superintendent alone for a few days.

Villard had made his preparations to start with a strange sinking at the heart. He was not a man to indulge in silly presentiment, but he could not feel any enthusiasm about going. He had not taken two days away from the

mills in two years, and was justly entitled to a
vacation ; but every time he thought of going
to Holyoke, his heart sank within him.

He thought it was because he must leave
Salome, and chided himself for his sentimental
fancies. He told himself to be a man ; not a
silly fool. And, finally, he refused to think of
his premeditated journey, since he could not do
so comfortably.

He was to leave Shepardtown on a seven-
thirty express, west. Salome remained at
the office unusually late that afternoon. She
made him go carefully over her various duties,
and recount, over and over again, everything
necessary for her to say or do while he was
gone.

The other superintendent was called away
early, and she was left alone with Villard in the
inner office, the clerks coming in and out and
Marion dropping in once on a trifling errand.

Finally, she said :

" Well, I suppose I must bid you good-bye.
I hope you won't be gone long."

She held out her hand and Villard took it.
A subtle fire shot from it straight to Villard's
heart. He looked up. Were her eyes, so soft

and kind, suffused with tears ? Was this the strong, self-reliant Salome ?

" Miss Shepard, Salome," he burst out, incoherently, " I——"

" Come right in this way," said a hearty voice at the other door. " Villard will tell you what you want to know——"

" Good-bye," said Salome again, in the most matter-of-fact tone, releasing her hand just in time, as the other superintendent ushered in a buyer from the west. " Good-bye and good luck ; " and turning, she walked away with the nonchalant air which a woman knows so well how to assume, even at the most serious moment of her life.

Poor Villard was both confused and exalted by the sudden dawn of blessedness, which had as suddenly faded. He turned to the buyer but was incoherent, and gave wrong prices on the last shipment of cotton, so that his customer felt obliged to call him back to his senses by a not over-delicate allusion to the parting he was shrewd enough to guess he had interrupted.

Salome went home in a strangely depressed mood. She ate but little dinner, and excusing

herself early in the evening on the plea of
unusual weariness, she retired to her room, un-
dressed and donned a silken night-wrapper,
only to lie awake all night, worrying herself
with fruitless questioning. In the watches of
the night and under cover of the dark, she
told herself that she had given her heart un-
sought; that had Villard loved her as she did
him, nothing could have kept him from saying
so; that she had been vain and conceited in
fancying that, under his quiet demeanor, he
loved her.

Then she remembered his sudden, yearning
look when he had grasped her hand, and that,
from the depths of his great, manly heart, he
had called her " Salome." And then, woman-
like, she shed a few hot tears of gratitude and
impatience.

Marion Shaw, meanwhile, had gone to the
Hall alone that evening. Her work among
the mill-girls had grown dearer to her heart
with every month. Most of the girls loved
her now, and looked upon her as a comrade,
though walking on much higher ground
than they. Many of them had secret aspirations to reach the standard of her ideals, as

they dimly conceived it, and were the better for trying.

Marion had not had a long fight with herself when weeks had rolled into months, and she heard no word from Burnham.

She had always been an individual girl—one who thought for herself, who set high ideals for herself, who believed that one only does one's duty by living at one's highest and noblest.

When she was a mere girl she had become acquainted with a young college-student, and their friendship ripened into love. When she became engaged to Ralph Leland, Marion looked upon her betrothal as no less sacred than a marriage vow. When, after a few years of study and close confinement in a theological seminary, Leland had shown symptoms of consumption and been ordered to Colorado, her mother was slowly nearing her death, with the same disease. It had wrung her heart with anguish to decide between them, but Leland had said:

"Stay with your mother, Marion. She cannot live long and needs you with her to the end. I shall live many years, and, I feel confident, may yet entirely recover. It is hard, but your mother can have but a year or two at the most. I hope to live for many years. And we could neither of us be happy if we remembered her here, sorrowing and suffering alone."

And so Marion had staid to nurse her dying mother, and Ralph Leland had gone west to seek health and strength. In two months he was seized with congestion of the lungs and died suddenly, away from all friends and apart from her.

What Marion suffered at this time, only a woman can understand. What she endured, only a woman who has gone down into the blackness of despair can conceive. Her mother failing gradually, her lover gone, what wonder that, for a time, life seemed a blank?

After the first, she had not talked about Ralph, but nursed his memory silently, day and night. For eighteen months, she took sole care of her mother, seeing her slip away into the "great unknown," inch by inch. Never did the mother realize that she was going to die, and she constantly made plans for the next season when she was going to be "so much better." Often Marion, knowing she

was soon to be motherless, would leave her low
seat near her mother, and stand behind the
invalid's chair to hide the tears that welled
up, even while she agreed with the invalid's
plans.

Day by day, the gnawing agony of seeing
her mother slowly dying before her melted
into and overshadowed the loss of that love
which was to have shielded and defended her
till death. But she never gave way, before
mortal eyes, to her sorrow; and she never
failed to minister to the mother who so needed
her care.

By and by she was left alone. Then, for
the first time, did the awful sense of loss over-
power her. For days she did not sleep or
take any nourishment. Then she rallied and
girded herself for the struggle for existence
which such women must make, and which, in
her case, had been eased by the door which
Salome had opened to her.

Through all her trials and discouragement,
Ralph Leland had been a present reality to her.
Even since the first blackness of darkness she
had believed that somewhere, somehow, she
would meet him as of old, and they would live

again for each other. Then she came to believe that he loved her still, wherever in God's great universe he might be.

"When he was in Colorado," she used to say to herself, "I never had a doubt that he loved me still. If he had gone to the farthest corner of the earth I should not have dreamed of his forgetting me. Why should I now, when he has only gone to a remoter part of the universe?"

This thought was the one, calm, sustaining help to her in all her work. And in this belief she was strong to take up any burden which might be laid upon her.

When she came to Shepardtown and met Burnham, she had been struck by the subtle, strange resemblance to Ralph which she saw in him. It was more than the mere resemblance of feature. It was the resemblance of expression, of looks, of the intangible essence of life.

From this point on, so long as she came in daily contact with Burnham, she was fascinated by this ever-recurring resemblance; sometimes she was half-persuaded that it was Leland who talked or sang to her, and she sat watching him in dreamy remembrance of the old days, before her mother or Ralph had sickened. As she grew gradually to believe that Burnham loved her, she thanked Heaven that a good man's love was to brighten her life once more. When the veil was rent away, and she saw that Burnham was not the true, white-souled knight she had thought him, and realized that he was not the ideal she had believed and trusted in, she was surprised to find that she no longer loved him. And then she thought out the true solution.

On the night of Villard's departure, as has been said, Marion had gone to the work she most delighted in—her work among the girls. There were classes to be overlooked, and her own special one in singing to be taught. She was half through the musical hour, when she turned suddenly towards the door. There stood Geoffrey Burnham.

Afterwards she remembered how little feeling the sight of him caused her. But then she said pleasantly :

" Oh, won't you walk in and hear us sing ? My girls have made decided improvement since you heard us last," and she went on composedly with the class.

Burnham looked on wonderingly. As he

watched this self-possessed young woman, his old passion flamed up within him. He had never cared for her as at that moment. When the class was over, she advanced toward him.

"Aren't you going to shake hands with a fellow?" he said, holding out his own.

"Certainly," she said, without the least emotion. He would have retained his hold upon her hand, but she withdrew it, saying:

"To what accident are we indebted for this unexpected pleasure?"

"I came," he said, "on business. I must see Villard. But they tell me he won't be home for several days. There's a certain combination of forces we want to get him into, if possible."

"You won't, you know," laughed Marion, "unless it's for the good of the working-men."

"Well, it is," answered Burnham. "A society is being planned for Lowell, which will do for the operatives there something like that which Villard and Salome and you have been doing here. I said I would come down and consult with him to-night. Besides, I——can't you guess any other reason for my coming?"

"Oh, plenty of them," replied Marion indifferently. "I suppose you feel a friendship for all who were once your people, and rather want to see them once more."

"Not that, at all," said he significantly, determined now that she should hear him out. "Are you going home? May I walk down with you?".

Marion gave her permission and went for her wraps. She half felt what was coming, but she was strangely apathetic.

When they were out under the stars, the talk began in commonplaces; but Burnham soon veered it round where he chose.

"Why are you so cold?" he asked, half querulously.

"Cold?" she repeated, purposely misunderstanding him. "I'm not cold. This wrap I have on is warmer than it looks."

"And your heart,—is that?" retorted he.

Marion did not answer.

"You know I love you. I—know you once loved me," he went on, losing his head, as a consequence of her indifference. "Perhaps you resented my treating you as I did. Perhaps I didn't do right, going off that way, without a word; but I thought it better

so.　You see—my mother,—and I,—Marion
Shaw!"—he seized her hand, grasping it in
both his own—"will you marry me?"

Marion withdrew her hand.

It was cool, and she felt like a spectator at
stage theatricals which did not concern her.

"Marion, you did love me, you can't deny
it!" he said.　"What is the trouble?"

"I'm sorry you have brought this subject up
to-night," she said, gently.　"It had much
better have remained dead and buried."

"Marion Shaw, you shall not evade me so,"
retorted Burnham, led on by her steady refusal
to respond to his passion.　"You did love me
—I was sure of it—or else, you are the basest
of coquettes, and were playing with me.　And
now you are tired of me!"

"As you were of me!" she blazed out, now
roused into speech.　"Listen, since you dare
address me as you do.　I did not love you.
You thought I did.　I thought I did.　When
you found it convenient for some reason, I
neither know nor care what, to leave me without a word, I found, for the first time, that I
was only in love with *being* in love.　No,—wait
until I am through.　Ten years ago I became

engaged to the bravest and best and truest man that ever lived." Marion's voice broke, but she went on. "He died and I kept on loving his memory, loving him wherever he might be. When I met you, the striking resemblance you bore to him smote me like an electric shock. You seemed good and noble like him, and under the glamour of your constant presence and evident fancy for me, I allowed myself to drift into a sentimental feeling for you. I now see what that feeling was. It was only a love of being in love ; and you happened to be the one man I have met so far, and I hope the only one I shall ever meet, capable of calling that feeling out. You have compelled me to speak plainly. I hope you are satisfied. This is our gate. Miss Shepard has retired, but she will be glad to see you at the office in the morning. Good-night." And Marion left him standing rooted to the ground where she left him.

For a few days Burnham felt himself a badly used man. He had loved and his love had been trampled on, he said to himself.

He went back to Lowell the next day, promising to write Villard ; and a week after, when he had settled down at home again with his dainty and querulous mother, he went calmly over the ground of his defeat.

"She never did a more sensible thing in her life," he declared, as he lighted his pipe, at last. "It would have been an awful bore to have to live up to her ideal."

XIX.

THREE days passed at the mills with no special incident. To Salome they seemed the dullest she had ever known. For the first time, she discovered that the Shawsheen Mills and the condition of its operatives was not enough to satisfy the inmost longings of her heart, or to still its disquietude. Without the presence of John Villard, and the constant inspiration of his presence, life lost its zest and sparkle.

When the three days were over, Salome went to her pillow at night with a sense of relief. Until now, she had not realized what her position at the head of the mills might mean without Villard. She saw that without him she could have done little, and would have made many mistakes—a fact which it was good for her to realize. And then she remembered, with sudden terror, that he might leave her at any moment, as Burnham had done.

" He will be home in the morning," she said
to her disquieted heart, " and I will offer him
a share in the business. I will make him a
partner, and then I shall never lose him."
And even in the darkness of night and the
privacy of her own room, she resolutely put
away from herself any other contingency.

The morning dawned beautiful, fresh and
balmy, as only a spring morning late in May
can dawn in New England. Salome dressed
herself with unusual care. A strange, happy
feeling under-ran all her thoughts. She would
not think of him ; she would not look forward
to his coming ; but, for her, all the gladness of
the May morning, all the blossoming of spring
flowers, all the caroling of joyous birds, meant
only that Villard had arrived in Shepardtown
on the night express, and that she would see him
in an hour or two. She did not hurry her
preparations for breakfast,—this was such a
strange, delightful mood. She looked at her
own reflection in the mirror, thinking unconsciously of making herself fair for him. She
sang snatches of merry song from the last
comic opera, laughing to herself as she recalled
how her nurse used to forbid her singing before

the morning meal, and how she used to repeat, in a lugubrious tone, the old sign :

> " If you sing before breakfast,
> You'll cry before night."

And, still singing, she stopped at her aunt's room, only to find that everybody had gone downstairs before her.

Mrs. Soule and Marion were chatting pleasantly over their hot-house grapes when she entered the breakfast-room. The morning papers lay untouched beside Salome's plate. She took her place and leisurely pared an orange. Afterwards she remembered the time she wasted in cutting the peel into fantastic shapes.

" Has nobody looked at the papers?" she asked, after a while. "I declare, how self-absorbed we are growing. Who knows but the world has, half of it, come to an end, over night?"

She picked up one of the papers—the one which contained the most startling head-lines, the most sickening sensations. Opening it, her eyes became riveted to the front page. Her face paled. She grew whiter, but no one

noticed. When Marion looked up, the paper was
falling from Salome's hand, and she had fallen
back in her chair—faint, speechless with terror.

With a cry, Marion sprang to her side; but
Salome, by a tremendous effort, recovered herself.

"Read it," she gasped, "and tell me what
to do."

Marion picked up the paper, and read:

HORRIBLE ACCIDENT ON THE ALBANY ROAD.

THIRTEEN KILLED AND TWENTY WOUNDED.

TERRIBLE SLAUGHTER DUE TO CARELESSNESS.

PROMINENT BUSINESS MEN OF BOSTON AND SHEPARD-
TOWN AMONG THE INJURED.

Running her eye hastily down the column,
Marion gathered that the night express had
been crashed into by a heavy freight; that
both trains had been thrown off the track;
that many passengers had been killed, scalded,
mangled or bruised.

She looked quickly over the list of killed.
There were no familiar names; but at the head
of the wounded was:

"John Villard of Shepardtown. Fatally injured. Impossible to recover."

She turned to Salome, who was already leaving the table.

"Help me to get ready," she said. "I must go to him immediately." Marion marveled to see her so calm; but she knew only too well the anguish concealed in the woman's heart below.

"What is it? What are you going to do? Why does not some one tell me?" asked Mrs. Soule.

"Dear auntie," and Salome bent and kissed the fair, soft cheek, "there has been a terrible accident to the train that Mr. Villard was coming home on. I am going to him. He is dying." Then she left the room.

In less than an hour she was at the railway station, waiting for the train to Boston. At the last moment, Mrs. Soule, having recovered from the shock which the news had given her, had tried to dissuade her niece from going.

It seemed to her that this was the strangest thing her unaccountable niece had ever done. She really must remonstrate with her on the impropriety of her conduct. And seeing that Salome would not be restrained from making this erratic trip, she proposed to go, too, as chaperon. Only Salome must wait for the noon train, as she could not possibly get ready for an earlier one.

"The noon train!" exclaimed Salome, buttoning her gloves. "No, auntie, Mr. Villard may not live until then. I shall go to him at once. You forget that I am no longer a young girl. I am a business woman, and my chief assistant lies dying." She bent over and kissed her aunt, who was still remonstrating, and ran down the steps to the waiting carriage, where Marion had already taken her seat.

Marion, too, had offered to go with her; but Salome had only replied:

"No, dear. If you will take my place here, that is all I ask."

And when the train finally drew out of Shepardtown, and she had left her friend standing on the platform, she gave an involuntary sigh. Only the strong heart, which can best bear its grief alone, will understand her feeling.

The train had never seemed so slow to her. Strained and anxious with that nervous intensity which makes a woman waste her strength in a half-conscious physical effort to propel, by her own will-power, the great, unsympathetic, methodical engine, she sat straight up in her seat with heart and soul benumbed. Constantly before her, was the picture of John Villard —mangled, bleeding, dying—perhaps dead. Her brain reeled as she thought of him lying pale and cold in death.

She remembered how, only three days ago, he had clasped her hand and looked into her eyes; how he had called her " Salome," his voice deep and tender with emotion. Dead? No, it could not be. And still the long, unfeeling train stopped to take on its horde of passengers, or to let off a working-man or a school-girl.

The hour's ride to Boston seemed to her an eternity ; and when, at last, they rolled into the long, covered shed, Salome was first to reach the steps, and first to touch the platform.

Ordering a carriage, she was soon on her way across the city. But here again the slowness of her progress drove her nearly frantic. She called to the driver and told him she would double his fee if he caught the next train for the scene of the accident. He did not know what time that would be, but he accepted the offer and drove at such a rate of speed that an agent of the Humane Society ran after him to catch his number,—and did not succeed.

When they reached the Albany station, Salome threw him the smallest bill she had,— a two-dollar one,—and without waiting for the change, hastened to the ticket-office. It was beset with more than the usual crowd of curious questioners and eager passengers, whose plans the accident had thrown into confusion. It was some minutes before Salome could reach the window. She was about to turn away in despair when the agent recognized her.

"Let that lady pass, there," he said, author-itatively; and then Salome learned that a relief train had been sent early in the morning, that another would be starting in ten minutes, and that regular trains would be run in the course of an hour or two, "carrying by," at Jones's Crossing, where the accident had occurred.

"And the injured ones, are they still——" her voice failed her.

"They are still living," answered the agent. "But some of them are so badly hurt they must die. Stand back there, one minute," he

16

said to the crowd. " Well, I don't know, miss, whether you could go on the relief train. You might go out and ask, though they've shut down on the crowd."

Salome turned away. For the first time since breakfast a clear thought came into her brain. She went out to the train-gate.

No, they could not take any one. There were so many wanting to go, and they only took one car. Oh, a friend of the injured? Well, she must go to the division superintendent, or the general passenger agent. There was the " G. P. A." over there.

Salome walked over to the official designated, —a pleasant gentleman with kind eyes.

" I am Miss Shepard of Shepardtown," she said; " my chief superintendent is among the injured, and is probably dying. He has no friends, and I must get to him. Can you help me ? "

The official took out a little book, wrote her name on a blank pass, and handed it to her.

" Anything we can do for him or for you, Miss Shepard, we shall be glad to do. You needn't hesitate to ask. Your grandfather was once kind to me, when I was a poor boy."

The passenger agent hurried away to the

engine, giving some last orders, and Salome did not have a chance to thank him.

"You'll have to hurry, miss," a brakeman said who was standing near. "The train is going."

A moment later she was on the way for Jones's Crossing.

This train had the right of way and a clear track for some distance. They seemed to fly, as they sped out through the suburbs into the country beyond.

The bloom of the May morning was still on the tender, up-springing grass and the fresh foliage of the trees. Birds sang cheerfully on, in spite of the thundering engine on its way to the scene of woe. But there was no more beauty in the world for Salome.

Three or four physicians sat in the corner of the one baggage-car which they all occupied together, and, used as they were to scenes of death and suffering, talked indifferently of politics and the misdoings of Congress. The brakeman laughed as the conductor passed him with some trivial remark. To Salome it seemed that she alone, of all the world, cared because thirteen persons lay dead and twenty more were fatally injured, a few miles away.

Afterwards, when she saw the tenderness and courageous sympathy of these people among the suffering, she reversed her judgment.

A small woman in black sat at the opposite end of the car, and was the only other passenger.

"Who is that?" She stopped the conductor to ask the question, at last drawn out of her own sorrow by the pathetic attitude of the woman's figure.

"That's the engineer's mother. He is fatally hurt. He's the last of her five boys, and her sole dependence. It's pretty rough on her; but the boys won't let her suffer."

His words came like a reproach to her. What right had she, with all her wealth and friends and pleasures, to think of herself as the only suffering one? What was her sorrow, compared to that of this bereaved mother?

She felt an impulse to go over to the motionless figure and speak a word of comfort. And then she felt the train slacking up.

"We're almost there," the conductor said, as he passed her again.

When the train stopped, two of the physicians, having heard who she was, came forward with

offers of assistance. The others were kindly
aiding the pathetic old lady in black.

And then Salome found herself face to face
with such a scene as she had never even dreamed
of.

The public is, through the "enterprising"
journalistic system of the present day, already
too familiar with such scenes of sickening horror.
To Salome, this one came as the vivid realization of things she had hitherto carefully avoided
in the newspapers.

At first, she turned faint and sick at the
prospect. Several dead bodies lay plainly in
sight, partially covered with a blanket. The
living must first be cared for; and groans on
every side, from those who, even yet, had
not been extricated from the debris, told how
much still remained to be done.

"Tell me," she said, catching at the arm of a
doctor who had been on the ground since day-
break, "where is Mr. Villard?"

"Villard? Let's see—tall man? Dark
hair and full beard? Yes. He was removed
to the tavern over there an hour ago." And
he passed on to another sufferer.

Salome looked across the railroad track, in

the direction the physician had pointed. There
was a country store, a " tavern," and three or
four less pretentious buildings.

Hastily she clambered over the torn-up track,
down the embankment and across the narrow,
open field. There were no signs of life around
the group of houses. Everybody was at the
scene of the accident.

She walked into the tavern. It seemed to be
deserted. Through the narrow hall she could
see, at the end of the building, a dining-room ;
at one side was the office, where no one was in
view. The clerk heard her step, however, and
came hastily from the dining-room.

" Is there a Mr. Villard here ? "she began—
" a patient, from the accident?"

"There are three men upstairs who were
hurt," the clerk answered. " There's no one
here to tend office, or I'd show you up." .

"I must find him. Is there no one to show
me the way ? " she asked, impatient at this
last trivial delay.

" They're each in different rooms up there,"
was the reply. " Walk right up the stairs.
There's nurses up there. They'll tell you."

Salome turned up the narrow, dingy staircase. At the top there was no one in sight. Groans came from behind a closed door. Inside, she could hear voices, subdued to an undertone. In the absolute silence, she heard the word "amputation." Could this be Villard's room?

She leaned against the wall, unable to try that latch. While she stood there, helpless and dazed, she lifted her eyes to the opposite doorway. It was open.

Inside, there seemed to be no one. Certainly there was no attendant. She stepped forward and looked in. There, on the white, clean bed, lay the form of John Villard, his face whiter than the pillow it rested against, his dark hair contrasting strangely with his paleness.

With the sight, all the repressed love of the last two years swept over Salome like a resistless impulse. A hand seemed clutching at her heart. Her limbs seemed paralyzed; but in an instant she was beside the bed, looking down at the closed eyes. A terrible fear that he was dead swept over her. With an inarticulate groan, she knelt beside him and laid her hand against his face.

He opened his eyes and smiled faintly. He thought he had died and reached Heaven.

XX.

VILLARD'S convalescence was slow and tedious. When Salome had found him, his dislocated shoulder had been restored to place, and his broken ankle set. Then, as there were not nurses enough for the great need, he had been left alone.

What passed in that first ten minutes after Salome had found him is still a sacred memory between them. At last, she said, looking at him through wet eyes, "You must have a nurse."

"Oh, Salome, do not leave me," he answered; and his voice, weakened from his injuries and tender with the passion which, at last, he had not been afraid to declare, was like music to her heart.

She bent her blushing face upon the pillow beside him. "May I stay and take care of you?" she asked, softly.

"May you? Oh, Salome!"

Another silence fell between them. Both hearts were too full for words.

"Then we must be married to-day." Salome had waited a little for him to say it; but, man-like, he had not been thinking of the pro-prieties.

"I cannot leave you to hired nurses now," she murmured. "So, there is only this one way out of it."

"And a blessed way it is."

And so they were married, that bright May morning, amid scenes of anguish, and while Villard still hovered near the gates of death. And for weeks they remained at "Jones's Tavern," he ill, wretched, racked with pain; she, bearing the trials and discomforts of the place, vigils of long night-watches, the dull, dragging anxiety; and yet, there was never a happier or more blessed honeymoon.

When he was able to be moved on a stretcher, he was taken to Shepardtown. Their home-coming was a glad one, although it was necessarily quiet. Every operative in the mills had been at the station, when the train that bore the two who had done so much for them came steaming in. Salome nodded to many of them, with moist but happy eyes. But the family physician, who had met them in Boston, would allow of no hand-shaking.

"Time enough for that by and by," he told the men who stood foremost in the crowd. "Do you want to kill him?"

He could not prevent several of the strongest ones from stepping forward, however, and taking the stretcher in their own hands, and bearing Villard very gently to the waiting carriage.

"I never thought to enter this house so," Villard whispered to Salome, when he was carefully borne up the stairs in the Shepard mansion and placed tenderly in bed.

"Thank Heaven, you were permitted to come, even *so*," she replied, with a shudder. He had been so near Death's door, instead!

"I can't and won't say I approve of what you've done," said Mrs. Soule that night. "If you must marry him at all, I could not see why you should want to do it then and there. You might have waited, I think, and had such a wedding as befits a daughter of the Bourdillons. Besides, all this watching and care has pulled you down. You look pale and worn.

You'll lose your beauty before you are thirty-five."

Salome did not answer. These matters seemed so trivial.

"I suppose, at least, you'll give a reception when he gets well enough. You really owe it to society and your own position. All your father's, your mother's, and your own friends will expect it. You have planned for that, I suppose? Since you had no wedding gown, you ought to give Redfern *carte blanche* for your reception gown. Have you written them?"

"Auntie," said Salome, "John and I have been, in these past weeks, where we did not think of party gowns."

"No, I suppose there was not much at Jones's Crossing to remind you of them. But now, you certainly are thinking of one *now?*"

Salome sighed. There was really no use in expecting her little, exquisite, cameo-cut aunt to understand her.

"I suppose we may give some sort of reception. All my people are waiting anxiously to see John," she said.

"Factory-people!" exclaimed Mrs. Soule indignantly; but her niece had moved away.

It was several weeks later, when Villard was first able to come downstairs. As soon as possible for him to bear the excitement, the operatives were invited to the house one evening, and permitted to shake hands with the man whom they had always considered their friend, and to whom they had now become closely endeared. The marriage between him and Salome had, somehow, seemed to draw him closer to them. They were now his people as well as hers.

"This isn't going to take you away from us at the Hall?" said one of the young men during the evening. "Mr. Fales and Mr. Welman are good—but they are not you."

"I shall be there every evening," was Villard's reply. "I am much more anxious not to lose you than you can be not to lose me."

"I don't know about that," the younger one said.

When they had all gone away, and Marion had sent them both upstairs for the night, Salome drew her husband down to her favorite seat in a cosy bay-window, where the August moon was streaming in through vines and foliage, making a checkered radiance around them.

"John," she began, "I have a plan to tell you."

"What is it, dear?" he asked, drawing her head to his shoulder.

"I am going to retire from active business." She laughed softly.

"What *can* you mean?"

"Can't you see? I'm going to retire. You are now the head of the Shawsheen Mills."

Villard said nothing. In spite of the great love between them, he could not forget that she was wealthy nor that he was poor.

"I have to-day made over the entire mill-property to you," she went on. "I am not going to have it said that your wife has all the money and all the power, and that you are only her dependent."

"Salome! you dear, generous heart," said Villard brokenly; "I cannot accept." He felt that she had divined his sensitiveness, although she had been too delicate to speak of it. "I am poor, but I am not a beggar."

"And I, too, am proud," she replied, laying her hand on his cheek. "I will not have people saying that you are tied to a rich wife and are subject to her whims. Oh, I know how they talk; I have seen and heard them all my life! Why, they would say you were a fortune-hunter."

" You do not think so?" he asked, gently.

" Confess, dear," she answered him. " If it had not been for that, wouldn't you have spoken long ago?"

Villard pressed her closer.

"I came very near it, as it was," he said, presently. " But I could not bear to be thought that."

" I had the necessary papers made out this afternoon," she said after an eloquent silence, " when I was out. So you see the thing is done whether you will or not. You need have no hesitation. I still have a large fortune left, you know, from the Bourdillons."

" If it were anybody else in the world but my noble, generous wife," he began, "I would refuse, even now."

" If it were any one else but my noble husband," she replied, "I could not yield control of the mills, and all the plans I have cherished for the employes. But I know in whom I trust," and her eyes shone with wifely pride and affection.

"There are still so many things to do," said Villard, a little later. "I know I can always depend on you to help me."

"Oh, I am not laying down the work and retiring to the old life of idleness," was the reply. "I shall leave the management of the mills to their new owner. It's no part of a married woman's business to manage her husband's office. But I shall have all the more leisure left for doing good. I have no end of schemes to lay before you ; and, I have no doubt, you have wiser plans than mine."

"I am glad, on the whole," said Villard thoughtfully, "that you are going to have more freedom. You are tired and worn with watching and caring for me,—dear, blessed soul that you are. Your burdens, in the past two years, have been borne marvelously well. Any other woman would have given way long ago. But, after all, I am a selfish man."

"You, John !"

"Yes. I must confess, I want you all to myself, a part of the time."

"All I have and all I am, dear, is yours. And yet, I cannot help feeling that we have still a great work to do. Employers, on all sides, are looking to see us fail in our attempts. As we stand or fall, will factories outside of Shepardtown be benefited or injured."

"I remember what you once said, Salome. Your brave words were a watchword with me many a time when my courage was low."

"What were they?"

"'We want to show the world that the spirit of Him crucified may rule in a cotton-mill as fully as in the life of a saint.' My darling, nobody but you would have had the courage to say that. We will take the sentiment as our rule of life."

"And act on Rossetti's beautiful words," added Salome:

> " And though age wearies by the way,
>   And hearts break in the furrow,
> We'll sow the golden grain to-day,
>   The harvest reap to-morrow!
> Build up heroic lives, and all
>   Be like the sheathen saber,
> Ready to flash out at God's call,
>   Oh, Chivalry of Labor!"

And then they sat silent in the checkered moonlight.

THE END.

BOOKS

From the Press of the Arena Publishing Company.

The Rise of the Swiss Republic.

By W. D. McCRACKAN, A.M.

It contains over four hundred pages, printed from new and handsome type, on a fine quality of heavy paper. The margins are wide, and the volume is richly bound in cloth.

Price, postpaid, $3.00.

Sultan to Sultan.

By M. FRENCH-SHELDON (Bebe Bwana).

Being a thrilling account of a remarkable expedition to the Masai and other hostile tribes of East Africa, which was planned and commanded by this intrepid woman. **A Sumptuous Volume of Travels.** Handsomely illustrated; printed on coated paper and richly bound in African red silk-finished cloth.

Price, postpaid, $5.00.

The League of the Iroquois.

By BENJAMIN HATHAWAY.

It is instinct with good taste and poetic feeling, affluent of picturesque description and graceful portraiture, and its versification is fairly melodious. — *Harper's Magazine.*

Has the charm of Longfellow's "Hiawatha." — *Albany Evening Journal.*

Of rare excellence and beauty. — *American Wesleyan.*

Evinces fine qualities of imagination, and is distinguished by remarkable grace and fluency. — *Boston Gazette.*

The publication of this poem alone may well serve as a mile-post in marking the pathway of American literature. The work is a marvel of legendary lore, and will be appreciated by every earnest reader. — *Boston Times.*

Price, postpaid, cloth, $1.00; Red Line edition, $1.50.

For sale by all booksellers. Sent postpaid upon receipt of the price.

Arena Publishing Company,

Copley Square,   BOSTON, MASS.

BOOKS

From the Press of the Arena Publishing Company.

Songs.

By NEITH BOYCE. Illustrated with original drawings by ETHELWYN WELLS CONREY. A beautiful gift book. Bound in white and gold. Price, postpaid, $1.25.

The Finished Creation, and Other Poems.

By BENJAMIN HATHAWAY, author of "The League of the Iroquois," "Art Life," and other Poems. Handsomely bound in white parchment vellum, stamped in silver. Price, postpaid, $1.25.

Wit and Humor of the Bible.

By Rev. MARION D. SHUTTER, D.D. A brilliant and reverent treatise. Published only in cloth. Price, postpaid, $1.50.

Son of Man; or, Sequel to Evolution.

By CELESTIA ROOT LANG. Published only in cloth.

This work, in many respects, very remarkably discusses the next step in the Evolution of Man. It is in perfect touch with advanced Christian Evolutionary thought, but takes a step beyond the present position of Religion Leaders.

Price, postpaid, $1.25.

For sale by all booksellers. Sent postpaid upon receipt of the price.

Arena Publishing Company,

Copley Square, BOSTON, MASS.

BOOKS

From the Press of the Arena Publishing Company.

Along Shore with a Man of War.

By MARGUERITE DICKINS. A delightful story of travel, delightfully told, handsomely illustrated, and beautifully bound. Price, postpaid, $1.50.

Evolution.

Popular lectures by leading thinkers, delivered before the Brooklyn Ethical Association. This work is of inestimable value to the general reader who is interested in Evolution as applied to religious, scientific, and social themes. It is the joint work of a number of the foremost thinkers in America to-day. One volume, handsome cloth, illustrated, complete index. 408 pp. Price, postpaid, $2.00.

Sociology.

Popular lectures by eminent thinkers, delivered before the Brooklyn Ethical Association. This work is a companion volume to "Evolution," and presents the best thought of representative thinkers on social evolution. One volume, handsome cloth, with diagram and complete index. 412 pp. Price, postpaid, $2.00.

For sale by all booksellers. Sent postpaid upon receipt of the price.

Arena Publishing Company,

Copley Square,   BOSTON, MASS.

Books

From the Press of the Arena Publishing Company.

Is This Your Son, My Lord?

By HELEN H. GARDENER. The most powerful novel written by an American. A terrible *expose* of conventional immorality and hypocrisy. Price: paper, 50 cents; cloth, $1.00.

Pray You, Sir, Whose Daughter?

By HELEN H. GARDENER. A brilliant novel of to-day, dealing with social purity and the "age of consent" laws. Price: paper, 50 cents; cloth, $1.00.

A Spoil of Office.

A novel. By HAMLIN GARLAND. The truest picture of Western life that has appeared in American fiction. Price: paper, 50 cents; cloth, $1.00.

Lessons Learned from Other Lives.

By B. O. FLOWER.

There are fourteen biographies in this volume, dealing with the lives of Seneca and Epictetus, the great Roman philosophers; Joan of Arc, the warrior maid; Henry Clay, the statesman; Edwin Booth and Joseph Jefferson, the actors; John Howard Payne, William Cullen Bryant, Edgar Allan Poe, Alice and Phœbe Cary, and John G. Whittier, the poets; Alfred Russell Wallace, the scientist; Victor Hugo, the many-sided man of genius.

"The book sparkles with literary jewels." — *Christian Leader*, Cincinnati, Ohio.

Price: paper, 50 cents; cloth. $1.00.

For sale by all booksellers. Sent postpaid upon receipt of the price.

Arena Publishing Company,

Copley Square, BOSTON, MASS.

From the Press of the Arena Publishing Company.

The Dream Child.

A fascinating romance of two worlds. By FLORENCE HUNT-LEY. Price: paper, 50 cents; cloth, $1.00.

A Mute Confessor.

The romance of a Southern town. By WILL N. HARBEN, author of "White Marie," "Almost Persuaded," etc. Price: paper, 50 cents; cloth, $1.00.

Redbank; Life on a Southern Plantation.

By M. L. COWLES. A typical Southern story by a Southern woman. Price: paper, 00; cloth, $1.00.

Psychics. Facts and Theories.

By Rev. MINOT J. SAVAGE. A thoughtful discussion of Psychical problems. Price: paper, 50 cents; cloth, $1.00.

Civilization's Inferno: Studies in the Social Cellar.

By B. O. FLOWER. I. Introductory chapter. II. Society's Exiles. III. Two Hours in the Social Cellar. IV. The Democracy of Darkness. V. Why the Ishmaelites Multiply. VI. The Froth and the Dregs. VII. A Pilgrimage and a Vision. VIII. Some Facts and a Question. IX. What of the Morrow? Price: paper, 50 cents; cloth, $1.00.

For sale by all booksellers. Sent postpaid upon receipt of the price.

Arena Publishing Company,

Copley Square, BOSTON, MASS.

BOOKS

From the Press of the Arena Publishing Company.

Salome Shepard, Reformer.

By HELEN M. WINSLOW. A New England story.   Price: paper, 50 cents; cloth, $1.00.

The Law of Laws.

By S. B. WAIT.   The author takes advance metaphysical grounds on the origin, nature, and destiny of the soul.

"It is offered as a contribution to the thought of that unnumbered fraternity of spirit whose members are found wherever souls are sensitive to the impact of the truth and feel another's burden as their own."— *Author's Preface.*

256 pages; handsome cloth.   Price, postpaid, $1.50.

Life. A Novel.

By WILLIAM W. WHEELER.   A book of thrilling interest from cover to cover.

In the form of a novel called "LIFE," William W. Wheeler has put before the public some of the clearest statements of logical ideas regarding humanity's present aspects, its inherent and manifest powers, and its future, that we have ever read.   The book is strong, keen, powerful; running over with thought, so expressed as to clearly convey the author's ideas; everything is to the point, nothing superfluous—and for this it is specially admirable. — *The Boston Times.*

Price: paper, 50 cents; cloth, $1.00.

For sale by all booksellers. Sent postpaid upon receipt of the price.

Arena Publishing Company,

Copley Square,   BOSTON, MASS.

BOOKS

From the Press of the Arena Publishing Company.

COPLEY SQUARE SERIES.

I. Bond-Holders and Bread-Winners.

By S. S. KING, Esq., Kansas City, Kansas. The most powerful book of the year. Its argument is irresistible. You should read it.

> President L. L. POLK, National F. A. and I. U., says: "It should be placed in the hands of every voter of this country."

Price, postpaid, 25 cents; per hundred, $12.50.

II. Money, Land, and Transportation.

CONTENTS:

1. **A New Declaration of Rights.** *Hamlin Garland.*
2. **The Farmer, Investor, and the Railway.** *C. Wood Davis.*
3. **The Independent Party and Money at Cost.** *R. B. Hassell.*

Price, single copy, 25 cents; per hundred, $10.

III. Industrial Freedom. The Triple Demand of Labor.

CONTENTS:

1. **The Money Question.** *Hon. John Davis.*
2. **The Sub-Treasury Plan.** *C. C. Post.*
3. **The Railroad Problem.** *C. Wood Davis and Ex-Gov. Lionel A. Sheldon.*

Price, single copy, 25 cents; per hundred, $10.

For sale by all booksellers. Sent postpaid upon receipt of the price.

Arena Publishing Company,

Copley Square,   BOSTON, MASS.

www.ingramcontent.com/pod-product-compliance
Lightning Source LLC
Chambersburg PA
CBHW030640030726
47497CB00006B/1882